WAYS TO BE
EQUALLY HUMAN

WAYS TO BE EQUALLY HUMAN

LESLIE TATE

**This edition published in 2024
by Eyewear Publishing Ltd,
The Black Spring Press Group
Maida Vale imprint
London, United Kingdom**

Cover design by Edwin Smet
Typeset by Subash Raghu

ISBN 978-1-915406-52-1

www.blackspringpressgroup.com

For me, writing is an adventure. So I type something on screen, look at it, then change or delete by feel. The aim is for something immediate, but also tested repeatedly, then chopped and changed in order to achieve closure. It's not about ordering material, but reflecting experience as it is.

At the same time, I'm listening for the hard-to-reach phrase that bends the rules - though only so far. Words have their own way of putting things; something the writer learns to work with, moving between the original phrase and the standard 'filler'. It's a shifty business: stepping back, balancing, testing the ground, then taking my chances.

These lyrical essays are *objets trouvés* placed in a gallery as testers. They're edits or selections, rather than copies of life. Written by feel, they reshape the actual to serve the imaginary.

In the room where I write there's a large cupboard. From the outside it's a tall, functional box with white panels and brown drawers. Standing higher than my head, it feels like a room within a room. I call it my depository.

Knowing, as I do, what's inside, I'm aware of it as an archive. It's my holdall for payslips, bills, allowances, statements − all of them going back years − plus several loose-leaf folders containing paperwork itemising everything I own. It makes me think of inventories, last testaments and remaindered books.

The smaller drawers are full of printouts of stories and poems, stapled together and arranged by theme, interleaved with worksheets and lesson plans. They're what I have to show for years of teaching and later, as a manager, covering for absent staff. If I could drill down through the layers I'd come to a place where I was busy twelve hours a day, eating as I worked and taking phone messages as I unlocked doors and settled down classes. I was in permanent action mode, and the collection of papers symbolises my hyped-up life, then and now. They were my fuel.

The larger drawers resemble a mailsack. At first sight the papers are piled up like fallen leaves. They're ink-stained, and all higgledy-piggledy. But a closer look shows a pattern emerging. They're bits from a flowchart – a makeshift one with its own connections. The links are there, but easy to miss. It's a jigsaw and an album, and it backs up my life.

What follows is selective. It's one way of fitting those patterns together.

Rebel, Rebel

1.

Let's talk about public toilets, starting with motorway rest stops. Why them? Because they're busy, and divided by gender. And let's remember as I walk into the men's I'm wearing a dress. Of course, I feel in danger. Men take you on. I've been told several times, "You're in the wrong place luv." I remember a man insisting, even though I was shaking my head, that I should use the other door. And when a friend went in with me, he told me afterwards about the filthy looks that came my way.

I avoid men's eyes. I don't want to give any pumped-up male the excuse he's looking for. Especially as people can see I'm tall and straight-bodied with big hands and a large face – and although my grey hair has volume, my voice is male and I don't wear makeup. Being non-binary, I take it for granted that my gender is mixed, but I use the men's because I'm anatomically male. I'm no danger to anyone, but whichever toilet I choose I could be in trouble.

When I go into the men's I head for a cubicle. I'm telling myself not to rush, but my pulse is up and my hands are tingling. I keep my head high and imagine facing off aggressors, but really I want it over with as fast as possible. I was bullied at school so my main defence is spotting body language and preparing to run or locking myself in a cubicle. In my mind's eye I can see blood on the tiles.

I remember being inside a cubicle in a Welsh toilet. The area was full of flushing noises, piped music and whirring hand driers. I'd finished on the toilet and was watching the space beneath the door, hoping I could escape during a quiet period. But there was no let-up and in the end I simply had to walk out. As I took my place at the washbasins, I realised I was surrounded by football supporters. They were quietly pumped up and ready for action. Fortunately, their random footie talk kept them busy, so I quickly splashed my hands, shaking them dry as I left. Emerging was like walking free from a juvenile detention centre.

Toilets vary. I've been in them alone and a man enters, sees me, and walks straight out. When he comes back, I tell him it's the right place. The look I get is usually a combination of puzzlement, surprise and relief. In other toilets, all cubicles except one are out of action and I have to queue up wondering if someone is going to take a swing at me. And in some toilets the layout forces me to stand shoulder to shoulder at washstands or hand driers, bringing back memories of being knocked to the floor in the school changing rooms.

When I first came out in women's clothes, I avoided all public toilets. If I was going on a journey, I'd either drink nothing, risking dehydration, or hold on until I was desperate, increasing the pressure when I went. Not only did that generate anxiety, but it became stressful as age weakened my physical control. So now I drink a little and risk having to go. I've not been assaulted yet and probably won't see it coming if it happens. In any case, most men mind their own business. But of course, it's absurd that, of all places, at the age of 75, I'm not safe in a toilet.

....

From the start, my secret habit put me at risk. There was no knowing what might happen if I was caught. It also implied some sort of guilt. So, for much of the time I wasn't really there. It was as if I was a spy behind enemy lines. Every so often I'd be taken over by my other self, beginning in childhood when I sneaked my mother's underwear into my bedroom. Wearing tights in bed was softly electric. It was hot and cold all over, and exciting. I felt enchantingly girlie and looked-after. I could hear the words of *Living Doll* running through my head.

I was fascinated by nice girls in swimsuits. I'd collected their pictures, cut from newspapers, and hid them in my bedroom. Their faces were softly rounded and beautiful. They seemed so assured. I'd a feeling from their smiles that they enjoyed being looked at. I was their secret admirer who lived in hope but expected nothing. And I watched and I waited, dreaming of the time when their smiles would meet mine. I'd found my ideal.

All Things Bright and Beautiful

Moving with care among his concealments
he trawled to the bottom
beneath pure white cotton and folded linens
to draw out his pictures of carnival winners
and unaware beauties displaying on the beach.

Struck breathless by their gaze, he wondered if
they *knew*.

What would they say if, like Pygmalion,
they could step from the pedestal
and, smiling encouragement, lead him quietly
to somewhere out of sight?

Would they offer all: finger-guide, capture
and simple explanation, the light in the window
and envelope unsealed?

Or were they embarrassed, like parents caught
kissing, to have him looking in?

And did they, as angels, do this with intention,
to flesh themselves out
or simply because they could?

See them now in life, smiling and composed,

all day with him: their gaze, their reach,
and passions blown large (put there to test him),
great ache in cotton
for bits tucked under and goodness that awaits,
and things he'd never touch folded to his heart
beneath pure white linen
in an unmarked drawer.

Decades later, when I began to dress in front of family, the limit was the front door. Even then, if my children's friends came round, I wore trousers. I avoided windows and quick-changed before answering callers. My real life was under wraps; I needed the house as refuge.

When I started going out at night, one of my first visits was to an Islington pub on a TV night. In those days, terms such as 'TV' and 'passing' were coded signals, but I didn't use them. I wasn't going to be labelled and disliked secrecy, although I parked nearby so I could sneak into the pub unseen. Following instructions, I climbed a narrow flight of stairs with a voice in my head telling me to turn back – and when I found my group, I felt like an intruder. The room was full of girlie-girls. They were squeezed into tight skirts and heels and went by flowery female names, while I was wearing a long Kaftan-style robe with low-heeled shoes.

When asked, I introduced myself as 'Les'. Looking back, I realise that was my male marker. It distanced me from being ultra-fem and placed me outside the group. Later, when someone advised me to 'go the full way',

I distanced further. I didn't want surgery or hormones and felt like an isolate. In truth, I'd too many red lines. I'd not come for the chitchat or to exchange tips on nail varnish and I didn't want to be drawn into something clandestine. So, when one young, heavily made-up TV bought me a drink and started propositioning me, I left.

When I took these trips out, I felt alive. At the same time, like an actor, I was hiding behind my part. For instance, at a self-catering holiday home where I walked the lanes at night wearing a long white dress with a hood. When cars came towards me, I shrank back inside the hood and held my breath. I'd cloaked myself in strangeness and mystery, like a ghost. Fortunately, nobody stopped to ask if I wanted a lift. If they had, I'd have been struck dumb, like Harpo.

For years I planned my outings as a POW escapes. I'd scout the route beforehand then, on the night, I'd go without glasses, carrying my 'other-self' in a bag. Sometimes, as extra insurance, I'd 'underdress' – male outwards, female underneath – using car back seats or toilet cubicles as my changing rooms. Wherever I was, I'd an escape route ready, a backdoor exit or at least an excuse involving appearing on stage or raising money for charity. I knew there were stories of men like me jumping from windows or locking themselves in cupboards to avoid being found out. I'd seen female impersonators and gay male activists dressed to provoke and I'd listened to *Lola* and read about glam types and 'dowdy' transvestites who copied their mothers, but the way they all presented wasn't for me. Looking back now, I see that they *were* presented – in my mind and by society – as departures from the norm. The idea that I was different was tinged with denial.

So how did it change? I began to tell people and for a long time that was enough. I dressed at home and sneaked out at night undercover, went to plays like *M. Butterfly* dressed as a man, and played both sides of the gender game. I was and I wasn't. Everything about me was reversible. I couldn't be measured or pinned down and I lived in a world of mirrors where nothing was as it seemed.

And when telling people wasn't enough, I began to write, at first for myself in hermetic poems then in prose with Jungian references, developing into third-person narratives about epicene adolescents and the woman within. I read as well, discovering two-spirit cultures, third-sex stories, Kathoeys and Hijras. It helped. But as long as I kept it private, the words were sketchy and unfinished, and although they told my story, the person they referred to wasn't really me. If I was in the picture, it had been turned towards the wall.

....

So why did it take 50 years for me to come out? The answer is what comedians call point of view.

For a long time, my fallback position was simple. Living in the binary world, I saw myself as male. Inside I was different, but that wasn't me. The man I was in public didn't feel gendered. He had his CV –

teacher, manager, father – and behind that, his politics and poetry. As doer and fixer, he was who he was. At the same time there were other selves, for example the cross-dresser who I treated as a split-off personality, and the show girl in the mirror who I thought I'd grown out of.

Calling yourself male makes things simple. It's the default setting. Like white or straight it's not mentioned – and that makes it invisible. So as a manager I didn't stop to think, just got on with it. I was my own self-styled hero who took on impossible odds and could work non-stop for hours.

There's something unwieldy about being a man's man. The standard image is Ken, the Barbie playmate. Ken is stiff and muscly, but behind the mask he's a fantasy creature. I was the same. Right from the start my boy-fitness was connected to magic thinking where I'd fly over walls and stilt-walk between buildings. In the physical world, of course, boys were required to run and jump and shout and kick balls in people's faces. So I struggled to cut a figure, couldn't pull it off, and found my real self in impossible dreams.

In my mind's eye I'm still there with Plastic Man and X-Woman. My adventures included surprise transformations, invisibility, and strange connections. I could appear on-screen taking giant strides into battle. As The Crazy Ghost I exited the back of camera in a rage, chewing up my enemies. As Kali I decapitated them and hung them upside down from the moon.

Sometimes I ask myself if I put on women's clothes to hide the macho underneath. Am I a wolf in sheep's clothing or just a man in a dress?

The Road Less Travelled

The snowballs hurt.
Scooped from walls
and rolled like dough
they had V-2 powers
to home in on their target.

The boys called them ammo.

Each hit was a small step,
a call inside and walk to the block
while outside he was Oates leaving the tent
to head towards God

turning into history.

. . . .

I'm looking in the mirror asking myself, "Who's that?"
It's a snap reaction, but it comes from a deeper place. As
I look, I sense how some people must feel when they
first meet me. Doubtful, perhaps, but curious, wanting to ask questions, though unsure where to begin, or
shocked, maybe, and a little threatened. For some it's
so unexpected they need a second take; for others it's
a deliberate provocation. Of course, they say to themselves, it's absurd, A MAN IN A DRESS??? A tall man

at that, in floral leggings with no hips or breasts and no attempt at makeup or any kind of depilation.

Looked at that way I'm on my own, keeping up appearances. But behind the mask I'm divided. There's a persistent inner voice that claims I'm kidding myself – or worse, accuses me of fraud. And to prove the point I hear myself calling blokes 'mate' or joshing or punching out words, like they do. It's a kneejerk thing. I do it to connect, but at the same time it feels quite natural. So while half of me is watching and listening, my other half is in performance mode. I'm one of the boys.

Afterwards, I question who I am. Where am I on the spectrum, I wonder, and is gender forever fixed, or is it performative? Certainly, there's a scripted feel about it, something so practised it becomes second nature. And once it's automatic, we don't have to ask questions. The world is – and always has been – either/ or. It's as simple as that.

Or at least, that's one way of looking at it. The opposite is less defined; more open-ended – a quiet blending of me with 'the other'. It's how I find myself, in present tense, both floaty and real. And as I walk down the street there's nothing hidden or to be afraid of. I'm fully alive.

Sometimes I feel the binary is a trick to keep us permanently pumped-up and preoccupied. Being sexy raises the bar: it's glam and intoxicating and attention-getting, and it seems to offer a kind of magic shield. But like all drugs, when its power wears off the only answer is to up the ante – and the more extreme it gets, the less it satisfies. In the end, it becomes a yawn.

I return to my mirror image. I'm a child again, wishing I was beautiful. I'm smiling. I want people to love me.

There's a doubt at the heart of being genderqueer. It's a part of what we all experience, but the questions go deeper. There's a kind of urgency about it, so it can't be ignored. I recognised this when I went to a meeting with other non-binary people. Everyone had their own preferred ID, often multiple, mixing trans with queer or non-binary, plus a range of pronouns – he, she, they, or simply a first name. But what I also realised was that everyone had their inner demon, like me, asking those questions. It's that part of us that won't lie down. I call it my *mirror-man* – lots of men, in fact, ganging up and speaking out of turn, casting shade on who we really are.

The task is to re-educate them.

Bildungsroman

It happened in the middle of a sentence
with a tap on the shoulder
and a voice from the past saying,
"Come with me." It was my story
told by the quiet stranger who walks beside us
on the road to judgement. The history of Queer –
from dives in the playground to midnight parades
in stolen clothes and makeup.
It continued as a passion
concealed behind a lip curl and a look
then a quick step away to prepare my answers.

I didn't say much. In the book I was writing
there were no leads or giveaways.
Behind the words were the acts of transgression
and self-as-other where the story stopped.
It wasn't like that or *it didn't really happen.*

I'd read about the man, caught in heels,
who jumped to his death.
The boy in a bra wired up for shocks.
The husband whose family had him committed
and the deep-voiced woman forced against a wall.
Like them, I had no one, unless my Mx
companion – whose name I'd missed – was me.

As the blows rained down, I closed my eyes
and pictured myself as the one that got away.

I marvelled, too, at the bar-top dancers,
the epicene boys in mascara and frocks,
the short-haired muscly women in black
leather jackets and the sweet-faced girls
who changed at dawn into warriors.
They were in love with the Gods.

Made like them I followed the whole story
with the voice of my guide in my ear.
"Remember," Mx said,
pointing to the squat figurines
with phallus and breasts and the two-spirit
Earth-protector poets speaking their truth
to the tribe.

And I heard and I grew and lived my life
in a shaped-changed HEA story

and didn't come of age.

....

I recently read *Two-Spirit People*, a collection of essays about 'Native American Gender Identity, Sexuality and Spirituality'. My aim was to investigate how other societies have viewed people like me. It was a dryly academic collection of essays but well researched, featuring several papers written by indigenous people. The book describes the diverse, multi-gender patterns accepted among the North American tribes, who based their societies on a different idea of what it is to be human.

Two-Spirit People begins by exploding the label *Berdache*, a term used by Western anthropologists for so-called passive homosexuals who wore women's clothes. In fact their clothes, though differentiated, were less binary than in the West, and their roles more varied. Personal identity in N. America sprang from what you did plus your spirit life, not from biology. It was common for women to take hunting roles because of gender imbalance in tribes and *Two-Spirit* people were sometimes regarded as doctors, poets and mystics. That changed during the twentieth century under the influence of Western thinking, so 'gender-bending' was seen as tainted by many indigenous groups and its existence denied in interviews. But before that there were records of people switching gender and developing intermediate genders (with a male to female bias that may reflect the researchers' POV or a society that takes more note of men than women). Also, there were same-sex pairings that were regarded as heterosexual. The key was usually a person's spirit identity. If two men or two women were together but one had an opposite-gendered soul then they were regarded as 'straight'. Having said that, the different tribes' cross-gender and multi-gender behaviour, which so shocked the missionaries, took many different forms. The label *Two-Spirit* was adopted as closer to the Native American model, rather than a Western LGBTQ+ perspective. In several personal stories N. American indigenous people described a wish to reconnect with their tribal roots after going through a gay liberation phase.

So what did I take away from the book? Firstly, I realised that that the term *Two-Spirit* has to be understood in context. It's wrong to appropriate it, but it does suggest that cross-gender behaviour was OK in the past. Secondly, the book hints that even before colonial thinking set in, there were times *Two-Spirit* people faced discrimination from their peers – while, paradoxically, being treated as mouthpieces for the Gods. It's an ambivalence that drives contemporary fears of gender fluidity. Thirdly, these stories are a reminder that our Western materialistic and reductive ideas of humanness are a narrowing of life.

....

"What are you, man or woman...?"

It was Friday lunchtime and I was with a group outside Barclays speaking to people about fossil fuels. We'd been inside, acted a die-in, filled the pavement with bodies and placards and been taped off by the police. It looked like a crime scene. Now we were preparing for part two of our protest.

The question – or statement – came from a young overweight spectator-man standing at the front of the crowd. He was staring at me with a dirty grin. I could picture him ogling girls and winding up kids at school

Behind me, two demonstrators, one male, one female, were kneeling in front of a large black-and-white sign. They were getting ready.

My answer popped out without thinking. "Neither."

Part of me had always considered myself male, softened by the non-binary label, but to be *neither* took it further. I'd become myself, a resister picked out by my difference. I could hear in my mind the words of Where the Streets Have No Name.

It had happened before. I'd been called a lady – sarcastically, aimed from behind – whistled and shouted at, and once, kerb crawled while shopping. Being catcalled was no surprise and the man in the van was a Bluto-type, but it took some getting used to. It was a lesson in what women had to put up with.

"Wha' the fuck," my spectator-man said.

In my head, I completed his phrase with ...*are you?*

A thin woman in a red top stepped up to the kneeling demonstrators. She was holding a bottle of thick, dark liquid.

"Climate breakdown," I called. "This bank funds it."

I stared at the man. With his bristly chin and leery expression, he was acting a part. I could see him in later life, leaning on a bar and swearing at women on TV.

"Crazy," he said, screwing one finger into his temple.

Behind me, the woman had raised her bottle to head height. As the spectator-man glared, my thoughts flashed back to a bully at school. It was all about swagger and overstated gesture. There was nothing underneath.

"F… F… bank," the woman called, anointing the protestor's head.

As the liquid oozed across flesh, the spectator-man laughed. "Weird," he shouted, waving one arm. "Weirdo man. Weirdo people." Choosing his moment, he began to walk away.

"No. Beautiful," I said, as the liquid spread like gravy. "But also… not beautiful," I called as it hardened to a crust. "Neither, really," I added. "Just human and wanting to live." In my mind I heard the phrase *That's why I'm here*.

His question had been answered.

....

Sue, my wife, calls me her beautiful boy. When she says that I feel warm and cared-for. It takes me back to the words of *With a Song in My Heart*. I'm the child at the front of the family photo. I've an ice cream in my hand and I'm smiling. The softness of my features makes some adults ask me if I'm a girl. Although I answer 'no', secretly it makes me happy to be asked. I like the idea of being in between. It's unusual I know, but I'm telling myself a story where I go to the ball in a gown and slippers. When I switch to playing The Handsome

Prince I'm actually a girl, acting the part. In the books I'm reading, I'm a tomboy, riding a bike and climbing trees, and when I get home I put on a dress. At school I sit with the girls and learn cat's cradle. Dressed as a girl, nobody can see me or touch me or call out nasty names.

Later in my teens, I'm reading Tolstoy's *Childhood, Boyhood, Youth* collected in one volume. I've chosen it because I'm trying to understand how boys become men. I try to go about my own business, act 'adult', and not show weakness. I'm learning how to give nothing away. Even then, secretly, I want to be admired. There are words I'd like to use such as 'beautiful' and 'lovely'. In my mind I can hear Maria singing *I Feel Pretty*. She's looking in the mirror and seeing me.

For a long time my beautiful boy stayed in hiding. I kept myself busy, making things happen. The aim was to impress. If I could stay calm and solid and remain on top while doing the business, then I'd be safe and no one could touch me. That way, I'd be a man and my real self wouldn't show. But for anyone looking closely, I wasn't what I seemed. Like Gulliver, I'd a thousand tiny threads tying me down. My heart wasn't in it.

I come back to how it started. I see myself as the high-voiced child singing to family, switching to a girl in secret, pouting. Now, I'm the boy with wings reading *Ode to a Nightingale*. And now I'm the pre-pubescent girl with smooth skin and false breasts. I'm tingling all over as I walk out at night in a dress. Later, I'm the man who switches gender in the middle of Chopin. Who understudies Bowie and smiles listening to *Rebel, Rebel*. It's about changes, switches, renewals, transformations.

Because I'm still Sue's beautiful boy.

Do Angels Have Gender?

The angle of his arm and thrown-out hand
is a bird of paradise flower where the sunbirds
land.

She's in orange and black. In a blue-green softness
of love burning down, the hotness

and ache of blanched skin are he/she/they
seen through a glass darkly. If this is the way

of all flesh, root and flower of unnamed self,
then with what wings do angels dance their
death?

2.

I'm sitting in the front row of Questors Theatre wearing red leggings and a couple of shorty vests covered by a slip. The slip is shiny and black; it shows my shoulders and arms – which at my age I usually cover up – while enclosing me in a cool sheath. It's simple, cut straight above my chest and knees, and made for theatre.

So, what am I doing here?

It's a 'summerslam' event, with twelve contestants ready to take the stage and present their two-minute monologues about diversity and inclusion. We're sitting in order of appearance, like prize-day pupils. I'm third, much the oldest, with no experience of delivering lines, and wishing I'd ducked out.

I'd prepared at home with words on paper, typed out in full then cut and shaped over weeks of silent reading and out-loud rehearsals, but what I'd finally realised was that using my script as a prompt wasn't enough. In fact, it was more like a journey down a road that kept giving out. One minute I was on track, the next I'd lost my way. So my daily run-throughs were stop-go exercises, beginning smoothly then pausing as I checked my paper, before delivering a few more lines, then breaking off altogether as I realised I'd muddled something or missed out a section.

But on good days, when the words came naturally, I'd reel off the first few sentences, easily, at one go. They went like this:

"At five I'd dreamed I'd been marched to the woods by rough boys and tied to a tree dressed as a girl. I was two-spirit, lovely, floaty, free and NOT TO BLAME. Afterwards my parents were SORRY FOR ME because I'd nearly died. And at school people treated me nicely because you DON'T HIT GIRLS."

The aim, of course, was to shock. It was a grand first statement: something so direct and truthful that no one could ignore it. But as I stood there, gesturing, I could see the child I'd been – an awkward, white-faced boy smiling seriously – and I felt for that child, staring in the mirror trying to look brave.

My script went on:

"Then at school the boys called me 'nipple' and dared me to fight or spit or wee up walls, then threw me to the ground and JABBED A COMPASS NEEDLE INTO MY ARM. But at home, when my parents were out, I'd get shouty. The devil was ordering me to get into my mother's underwear drawer AND DRESS LIKE A VAMP while my angel-self pleaded, 'No-no, that's not you'. I sinned, of course."

At the mention of sin, my voice dropped. I'd been on my own, a lost boy posing in a skirt, smiling his come-ons. A Narcissus-type, locked up in himself. And the figure in the mirror was partly me in ceremonial garb and partly an unreal stranger: I'd marked myself as not of this world.

But my voice lifted at the end-phrase 'of course'. I was smiling at my childish dramas and inviting the audience to join me. It was as if I was looking back from a dark space in a can't-catch-me film, waving at my accusers.

My piece continued:

"In the bath I'd squeeze my willie backwards behind my legs to look smooth and clean and curvy. Later, as a father, I dressed at home BUT DUCKED BENEATH THE WINDOW WHEN PEOPLE CAME BY – and kept my girlie self at arm's length."

At that point I pulled down my slip to show my breasts. They were small but prominent like moulded wax. Cupping one in my hand, I smiled, while my speech ran on, echoing strangely like a radio in my head…

So now, I'm sitting in Questors Theatre checking my script. It's small-print, typed on card and fits in one hand. It reminds me of my childhood magic tricks. Like them, I try to keep it hidden.

As my monologue approaches, my legs get restless. I try distracting myself by gazing at the empty stage with its brightly-lit centre spot. Behind me, in the tiered auditorium, the audience are chatting and shifting about. As five people enter from behind a screen, the lights dim and the voices stop. It's the judges, who take the front row in what looks like a pre-arranged order. The woman in the middle, wearing a red silk scarf and heels, takes her place first. It's almost as if the others have to wait for her before sitting.

When the first monologue begins, I realise I'm not going to win. The actor is young; he speaks conversationally with his eyes raised, talking to the back row as if he knows them well. He has lift and range and presence. He's followed by a woman reciting Lorca in a singsong voice. She, too, has a direct line of contact with the audience. Neither of them pause, or appear to be lost for words. In fact, they don't seem to be actors at all but real live, face-to-face characters introducing themselves. When it's my turn I take my place on stage. I've been warned that I'll be timed out by a bell so I start straightaway. There's a small part of me on fast forward running through my speech; the rest of me is in action mode, delivering it. I'm both performer and prompt, and my voice leads me, going high, going low, as I work the changes. And yes, it is a performance;

I'm here on the spot, but also somewhere else, and my words fill the gap between me and the audience.

But I get through it, and towards the end I hear my voice rising, projecting to the back row. The bell rings and I squeeze in a few last words before sitting down. It's a relief to be finished and the burst of applause surprises me, bringing me back to myself. Inwardly I've blanked, but outwardly I've joined the audience as an observer. So when the next actor is called I listen without trying to rate her. It's a practised piece, full of powerful social commentary. When she finishes, her place is taken by another actor and another, until the monologues end and the judges retire. Their exit marks the end of the summerslam for the performers. It's a weight off my shoulders, almost as if the contest had never happened.

In the interval I put myself around, talking to the actors. I'm in listening mode, collecting ideas for writing up the show. I ask them about learning lines and speaking with passion, and putting the two together. Their answers are various.

One actor uses a long mirror to practise her role, another drills herself to learn the words first, minus expression, a man uses repeat-chanting to music, another isolates passages and keeps re-reading; there are body-types who link words with actions and out-of-body types who just do it and chameleon-types who hide behind their words - they all have their own worked-out private routines. But what strikes me, mostly, is how they take to it naturally, without thought, like swimming or dancing, and just keep going and going...

And now, looking back, what did I learn?

- Acting is a branch of self-observation, practised obsessively like a top-level sport.
- Getting up on stage blurs the boundary between truth and illusion, creating its own special form of magic thinking.
- It's a way of being; a fine-art form and a gift.
- Playing a part requires more than a few weeks' solo practice.
- Acting isn't about the self-styled performer who overcomes impossible odds or the self-appointed talent stepping on stage to outdo the professionals. It's a meditative discipline that comes from the soul.
- My attempt to act was once-and-once-only.

And what happened, when the judges returned? The winner was announced, the runner-up was named, thanks were given and the chosen actors were applauded.

I was glad I didn't get a mention.

And the words at the end of my speech?

"But now I'm old and look, I've got breasts. They're hard and they hurt. It's the male menopause with fatigue and depression, aches all over, sleep-loss, muscle wastage.

But I'm still that girlie-boy, two-spirit person in the woods."

3.

I was a theatrical child. Beginning early, I hid my dramas behind a peepy smile. I'd a world to get used to where anything could happen. There were people in disguise and guardian angels watching every move. They could see right through me. My aim was to be like them to escape all notice. So, to head off danger, I filled the house with stories. And, by filling every corner, I put myself in charge and built my defences. Because I knew there was a place where everything was different. A land that faced away. And I was the child performer whistling in the dark.

What's beneath the stairs?
Mr Hoover and Mrs Brush.
Old Lino and his pipes.

What's beneath the sink?
McOrange Bowl and Squeezy,
with Grandma Basket and lots of little Pegs.

What's in the shed?
The Rust Lamp Shift and Hosepipe Squad with
Huge Policeman Fork.

What's in the sideboard?
Lord and Lady Silver with Tea Sets for the family.

What's beneath the bed?
The Trunk Man and Old Shoe Woman.

What's in the bathroom?
Soft Soap and Flannel with their stories.

What's on the coat stand?
Grizzly on branches.

What's in the locked drawer?
Dr Cough and his medicine. The Rev Crucifix.
Messrs Underfelt and Cloth.

And what's at the window
caught crouched forward in buttoned pyjamas
lit by the moon?

Later, in the car, I played games. They were my *let's
pretend* shows. Like people and pets, they came in different sizes. As OCD actions, they filled up my mind.

In game one, I was a sweet-toothed animal. It was in
my nature. So far, I'd been lucky and not been spotted. The
danger was I'd be flushed out and end up running wild.

In game two, I was on the launchpad, counting
down. My dad was the pilot; Mum read the maps.
When the traffic stopped, I'd be shot from a cannon to
scout the road ahead.

In game three, although no one noticed, I was the
diver in a cage who'd gone back in time. I'd just come
on land and was counting up lifeforms. Part of me was
excited, part was holding my breath.

So what had I become, and where was I going? And
was I what I seemed?

Animal, Vegetable, Mineral

It's an animal. Eats sweets.
Hasn't got a tail. *Inside* the car.
Sits still all day on the long ride north.
Has a wet patch, hidden. Doesn't have a name.

Can be animal; can be nice too, or better.
Mustn't say what. Or touch things.
Holds in smells.

Names the different cars. Knows the route well.
Wants to fly a plane. Counts up legs on signs.
Plays twenty questions.
Doesn't like vegetables. Dreams of coming first.
Can scent the sea – it's in everything.
All day looking forward.

The drive to the seaside was slow. I looked out for signs and counted off the miles, but when the road numbers changed, the distances changed too. It reminded me of when we put the clocks back. So when we reached my grandparents, I was still counting. But when they came out to greet us, I smiled. I'd read about homing pigeons and cats that came back and could feel something similar. I could tell my mum liked it, my dad cheered up and in my heart of hearts I knew the grandparents loved me.

They were artistic. My grandpa conducted the Messiah and gave speeches at Christmas; my granny played Bach on the organ. The house they lived in was their gallery. It was high-ceilinged, with open coal fires and framed family portraits. There were shells on the mantlepiece, flowers in vases and a ship's barometer by the front door. They lived on a road that led to the beach, and we trekked there daily to camp out on the sands. It was cold and exposed and we picnicked with our coats on. After putting up the tent, my dad took me exploring. We dug out trenches and built dams against the tide. When my mum joined us, I collected pebbles, filled buckets with shrimps and stick-drew messages in wet sand. When I paddled barefoot in the sea, I could see all the way to the horizon.

I began counting again. This time, in big numbers.

Time between tides
        steps to the lighthouse
                distance to China.

Trippers to the front
        drops in the ocean
                beats of a heart.

Shells against wood
        hairs on a head
                grains on the beach.

Ants in the yard
        pools between rocks
                pieces in a box.

Cards in a pack
        sweets in a jar
                seconds of a life.

Winner at crib
        wickets in the series
                speed of Donald Campbell.

Buttons in a tin
        notes of a symphony
                stars in the sky.

Wind at the flagpole
        wave crests breaking
                singing to family.

When we stayed there in winter, everything was different. The promenade was bare, the red flag was up and the shops shut early. When the waves came in, they broke across the road and filled up the basements. On still days when the foghorn boomed nobody went out. It was a kind of curfew.

So, what did I play then?

Sea bits in a jigsaw. The boat's quite simple.
Try that on the clock tower.
This way up for the flag on the green.
That belongs to the child, that's her ice cream,
strings to a kite, her windmill's in the corner.
Slides take effort, swings have a knack,
flowers can be boring.
The boy with the binoculars
appears in several places,
as do the golfers, as do walkers.
What about the dog? What's that he's chasing?
Maybe it's his tail?
And is that a bather? Or one of the family eating?
So many colours in the sea.
And seagulls everywhere, you can't tell them
from the wave crests, breaking.
The horizon's hard,
and just look at that sand.
Over here's a shelter, a bus stop, a fountain.
The fairground's just behind,
you can tell by its colours.
Bumper cars take skill,
the wheel's more difficult,
the dipper's impossible.
The sky's got so many pieces.
Can't see beyond that.

....

Back home, after watching tv, I put on crazy shows. I clowned in the mirror, gave orders to myself, imitated neighbours, and doubled myself in cartoonish monologues, delivered before sleep in the darkness of my room. My mind was full of it. One-act conversations, dingdongs and run-throughs with imaginary faces that just popped up. I'd sing as well, encouraged by visitors, then worm my way to the front of the family photo.

At birthday parties I'd go mad. I'd run around shouting, dance, bounce on beds, wave out of windows, play *can't catch me*, then fill myself up with crisps and lemonade. It was as if I was on power surge and couldn't switch off. When I did, I was sent to my room, crying.

Afterwards, I took myself off to hide in the garden. Playing the observer, I made out what I could. Ants on the path, blackbirds on the veg patch, caterpillars on leaves. With the house wall behind me, I dug myself in. The world was all around me; its names were on the tip of my tongue.

I played.

I spy beginning with I – small eye now,
bottom of the steps. Absorbed, unawares,
in ant lines running stone.

With B there, busy, blind spot to the house.

C, these are the facts.
Statements, opinions: behind them, the dark.

D-Day always, peering brickhole spiders
where words won't come.

E to H. Heart in mouth, keeping very still
as ridged on concrete, the daylight sleeps.

K's what knocks.
Mr Tall Bones. Mrs Bramble.
The Penknife Boys.

'LO, who's there?
Mars Man with Pop Ups. Chop, chop, chop.
Big Daddy Long Legs groping on wood.

M & N. No one.

OTT with visitors.

With U crouched down
where, silver and flaky, mortar scrapings
powder earth.

All V fingers. Now mix in water to a paste.

I again for fillings. Plaster. Layers in a cake.

ZZ for sleep. Push in more.

And now, looking back, were my games a slice of life
or a goofy self-parody? Was I sampling, pulling faces,

or trying to find myself? And was it an experiment or a mirror held up?

What I do know now, is my games were obsessive. And like my gender, hidden. They were the show behind the curtains and the boxed-up self hidden in a drawer. Inside their world I went undetected. I could shift between characters, plant secret messages and take on both sides.

I'm with that child now. I see him/her trying on costumes. There are feelings coming up: I'm trying to understand them. The world's close by and I'm on stage. It's a full dress rehearsal where I write all the lines, act as I like, and fancy myself up. It's an XYX theatre where anything's possible. And I'm in the thick of it.

A poem about my grandpa. Like me, he was starstruck. We shared a condition.

Dupuytren's Contracture When one or more
fingers bend in towards the palm - NHS

My grandfather, too.

For him, a railway clerk,
the tucked-in fingers,
lowered like handles,
were signals down.

Hard skin bumps, appearing slowly,
bubbled in his palm
like aphids on a leaf.

Or spoil heaps on a path.

Sometimes, when he sight-read,
he talked of chopping off.

Later, staring,
he saluted in the mirror
or rubbed them to a glow.

Most times, ignoring,
he led thumbs up,
then, arms out and smiling,
V-signed from the front
conducting the St Matthew

to a packed church hall.

Red-faced at the end
he gave thanks, stood waiting,
then held them up as roses.

Two up, two down, and counting.

To his choir they were fists.
Deadheads he called them,
as he knocked them into shape.

What made him and cheered him
and blocked him at keyboard
forced out song.

Squeezed to a stop
his hand turned down
like a fly in amber
or underfoot plant life
closing on itself.

Rising now, my flesh knows his mark.

As if some small mouth
or half-grown embryo
had entered into skin
leaving its intention
burrowed in a handshake.

My thoughts about writing begin with the image of a book as a house of cards. What I see is an interlocking structure where each word has to be added carefully, judging how much weight it can bear. If the words hold together they support each other, if they don't the whole caboodle comes tumbling down.

But to keep up that balancing act all the way is difficult. It's a long journey and a well-judged finish, whether it's a conclusion or a reveal, can make all the difference. It's what I look for when I read with a writer's eye, comparing the quality of the first and last pages.

Thinking more about the images that might fit a book, I came up with three more:

- A child's wordsearch conducted in a dark space.
- A high-wire performance where tiny adjustments make all the difference.
- An Impressionist portrait that captures the essence of its subject.

But the image that keeps coming back is the book as a symphony. Why? Partly it's the effort involved, but also its length, subdivisions and historical conventions. Because although a book appears to offer almost total freedom, those conventions still act as signposts and boundaries.

It's my Shout

In the landing cupboard I keep my vinyl. The records are packed on wall-to-wall shelves. It's a boxroom, really, a holdall for books and backpacks and recycled packaging. And like my cupboard it's full to bursting. The records are from all eras, beginning with Leadbelly and early Blues and ending with Suede and Britpop. A lot of them I replay in my head, although mainly highlights, because when I listen on the record player, I realise I've skipped key changes or connecting passages. It's how memory works. We hold onto edits from our past, using them as ID markers and backgrounding anything that doesn't fit our chosen story. But if we foreground different experiences, we change who we are.

My vinyl collection looks different today. I put it together as a personal resumé, a kind of private view. My albums were a big statement – a creative selection, marking me out as a left-field thinker. Today I see them as a critic's choice, slightly highbrow but not as underground or experimental as I thought they were. I wanted them as my own pet project, my opus. They were the proof that I would be recognised. Inside their covers were my hidden hopes of fame.

Later I came to see that some of them stood out as seminal. They were made for themselves, not with an eye on an audience, but in a space of their own. And, like children or poetry, no kind of valuation could be put on them.

1.

When I was at school poetry was taught by spotting similes, metaphors and other figures of speech. We memorised lines, rote-learned what the poet was 'doing' at various points in the text and copied out prose summaries of our set poems. We were also instructed in sonnet form, syllable-count and meter. It was all about displaying received knowledge and passing exams. Oddly, we didn't think to ask what was the purpose of a poem.

Outside the classroom the boys and their parents had a different idea. They believed they knew what a poem was about. It was a kind of puffed-up airy nonsense full of effete gestures and fancy language. Either that, or a poem made no sense at all and wasn't worth the paper it was written on.

Both approaches were summed up by the rhetorical question, 'What's the use of poetry?' Poetry was too much above our heads to be questioned or it was a complete waste of time. So we learned to get on with it in the classroom while admiring more down-to-earth things, like sport or earning money.

But what I remember was a sense of wonder. The similes and metaphors surprised me, and the poems had an inner wildness and strangeness that spoke of other things. And I lived that feeling, making it happen in the privacy of my bedroom, or on long walks, by whispering lines without understanding, casting myself as a Romantic poet and working myself up to a spiritual lather.

The best words in
the best order

This is a poem.

At 14 it was all over.
Following the lead of the voice from the front
I'd spotted metaphors
and made notes on wordplay and parts
tapping out rhythms in my head
as I walked through woods by the lake.

Autumn. Mud on pitches. Faces at the window;
the teacher talking mark schemes.

I wanted to pass. To walk it in beauty on my own
so high and bright that no one could touch me.

But the words brought me back.
When the teacher spoke, he wanted answers.
I wasn't ready, others got by.
We all knew his favourites, smart-aleck pleasers
who'd learned their lines well.
They filled the classroom with points score,
figures and the naming of devices.

Outside, on the field,
the countdown had begun.

Time was short. The light was fading.
Like leaves on grass our mistakes piled up.

My sadness was inside. I'd gone to ground
as I stepped off the path, closing the gap
between thought and action, to find what's me,
what's not.

The world was a nightbird in hiding.
It was hit and miss or too deep for tears
and we were under orders.

In the poem I'd started,
the sun glared red, mist wrapped the view,
the ice fields held the traveller.

All term, as I walked,
the woods were in my soul.
I'd written my goodbyes
and now was above it all,
holding up a book at the end-of-term service.
When my name was called,
I'd step forward and open it.
Reading on, I followed the boy-poet who
stole the boat and sailed off into otherness.
He was in everything.

Nobody was with me as I put aside my notes.
Heart in mouth, I was elsewhere.

Halfway through the questions
my words gave out.
When the marks came back I didn't dare look.
I wasn't in the running.

None of this/all of this is true.

The purpose of a poem seems very different to me today. It's closer to jazz or dance or mindful observation. Given that, what would I say to my younger self about poetry?

- It doesn't have any purpose at all if you try to measure it by money, work, exams or scoring goals. It can carry a 'message' or help with difficult feelings but its primary function is to be a thing of beauty, an elusive, affirmatory or shocking experience or a series of surprising expressions that cannot be adequately stated in other terms.
- But it does have music. In fact a poem 'stops making sense' only in so far as we require a single, logically-constructed meaning from language. A poem steers a middle path between grammar and the sound of words. To appreciate its unique voice you have to tune in, rather than irritably demand what on earth it's about.
- At the same time, it can be helpful to trace a thread of meaning through a poem. It won't be exhaustive and there will be ambiguities but it

provides a framework. The flower that grows on that framework is full of scent, colour and sharpness – and every day it changes.

- To interrogate a poem takes a lot of practice. It involves examining words carefully from all sides, trying to plot their moves and measure their connections. It's a matter of feel and practice and knowing about backgrounds and habits. It can involve the skills of a tracker.
- Poems are about metaphor. Recognising new similarities in a complex world.

So, taking apart a poem can be genuinely helpful if it offers a structure for thought and feeling that can be discarded later. The problem I have with my schooling was that by concentrating on technical effects we missed the heart of the poem. In our reductive, literalist classroom we were lacking the sense of strangeness, of deep connection and surprising meanings. Instead of allowing the poem to interpret us, we had the task of boxing it up and fitting it to a practical formula, one that would allow us to pass our exams. The purpose was external, lacking in the reflective or transformative process that poetry can and should initiate.

Hagiography

There were metaphors everywhere.

Learning was a long-distance run,
the headmaster said as we huddled on
benches fidgeting with our hymnbooks.
They were old, dogeared
and printed in Gothic script.

One cough and you were sent to his office.

Once, as I waited outside,
I imagined running in the snow.
If felt like being on pilgrimage. My legs ached.
The wind on my skin was an open wound.

Sitting in state behind his mahogany desk
the headmaster spoke. I was in deep;
he could see right through me.

As I lowered my gaze I remembered
the instructor ordering me to jump.

When the water hit me, my breath stopped.
Afterwards, sucking my fingers, I heard
someone say it was for my own good.

I'd been cast out.
All week in assembly, I hid my blushes
in a book. My feelings didn't matter.
Nothing would show if I held my breath.
Everything was real.

2.

Trying to be a poet wasn't easy. The boy had set his heart on it. Poetry was like reading lines from a prayer book, if you followed with your finger then good things might happen. But if you spoke out of turn or in the wrong order then it might strike you down. Poetry was a bit like walking alone or smelling flowers, it didn't win you friends. In fact, poetry was for weakies – that's what kids at school said. They hated having to study it. Why, they asked, didn't poetry just say what it meant? It was all the fault of stuck-up poets who spoke posh and needed some fist.

"Poetry stinks," said kid A, sniffing his fingers.

"Poetry's nothing," put in kid B, winking.

"Poetry's for poofs," kid C added, dropping his wrist.

But behind closed doors the boy kept the faith. He could see the hidden poet peeping out from the mirror. In his bedroom he recited lines from famous poets who, like him, had been loners. There was beauty in their sadness and truth in what they said. They were his companions who went with him everywhere. And when he walked out in the countryside, he heard them at his side.

"I'm the dream bird," the Poet of the Sky said. "My words have wings."

"Listen to me," said the Poet of the Wind. "Or I'll blow your house down."

"Kneel with me now," cried the Angel Poet. "For we have sinned."

Mostly, he just listened. He knew they were in his head, although in another way they were real. To have them with him as his guardians was good. So he walked through fields seeing signs in the clouds and hearing voices in the leaves. Like migrating birds, the poets were everywhere. The whole unseen world was in their hands. And the boy felt alive, and in touch with the dead.

....

The boy found his muse.

Elêgié lived inside the poetry book he carried in a pocket. Elêgié was a Kore who sang to the Moon. She was the woman wailing in Kubla Khan and Lucy in Wordsworth. Like him, she was wild.

"What's your name?" she asked him when no one was looking. They were walking together through bright spells and showers. When the rain came, they sheltered in a wood.

"Rima," he said.

"That's a beautiful name."

The boy looked down. He was mouthing words from his book.

"It's my name, too."

"Yours?

"Yes. Mine."

"We're the same?"

"Elêgié Rima."

Her voice had turned inward. It echoed in his mind and blended with the rain. When the rain stopped, they walked out again but this time into a glare where they couldn't see each other. It was as if they were actors in a spotlight. All connection was by feel, as they moved through scenery that looked like a painting.

They'd arrived at a moss-covered cave behind rocks. Stepping forward, they pushed through a screen of ivy. The chamber they entered was lit from above.

"Look," said Elêgié.

White flowers were hanging from the rock.

"Are they real?" asked Rima.

Elêgié smiled, "Touch one."

"It's an icicle," he said, fingering a floret.

Elêgié broke off a bit. It fizzed and crackled in her hand. "Taste it."

"Can I?"

"Try. Suck it. Like a lolly."

As Rima raised the ice to his lips, he felt a gentle radiance spreading around him. He sucked, and the glow became stronger. The walls of the cave seemed to be thinning out. It was as if everything about him was being stripped away.

Realising suddenly he was feeling sad, he returned the icicle to the wall. "Elêgié," he said as the figure before him faded. Repeating the name, he began a poem in his head. As he wrote he felt a gap extending everywhere. She had gone; the world was empty; this was what death must feel like.

....

Rima wanted to lose his sense of who he was. To step off down the street and melt into nothingness, like a ghost. It was a trick he'd learned from reading about undercover agents. He'd an invisibility lever inside him, together with a poem, hidden inside a box. In his dreams, when he removed the lid, the box became see-through, and when he pulled the lever he disappeared into something larger than himself.

He knew there were stories about boys who vanished and didn't come back. He'd seen them on posters looking sad, and he'd read about kidnaps and stow-aways – so he walked down the street without turning his head, listening for followers.

The poem was his magic passport. If he woke one morning and had lost his memory or was washed up exhausted on a beach, or if he'd wandered to a place where someone demanded ID, he'd recite his poem. It was his route map and polestar. And when the lights went out it doubled as a torch and lifesaver kit. Anything was possible. He could be transported back through time or find himself standing looking out on a scorched-earth landscape. And wherever he went, he was made one with nature.

Then he walked a long way out to the sea's edge. It was old and powerful. He could feel it moving inside him, like an animal in a dream. And for a while he was part of its cold rise and fall. But when the tide came in, he turned away.

Then Rima climbed to the top of a hill. Here he saw the land in map-view, laid out in folds. There were slopes down to rough patches, stunted trees, and sudden drops. In other directions it was green and smooth, like a carpet. A faint blue haze surrounded everything. But when the sun went in, his vision faded.

Rima tried other places. He looked out through a window at the stars. Moving side to side, he tried to judge their distance. Although they seemed so close, they were on journeys into nowhere. He knew that from books. In the daytime he followed clouds. They looked like Monet's waterlilies. Sometimes they broke up or bunched into massed growths, at other times they were armies, marching.

Then he tried tracing back a stream. Its surface was silver and shiny, like the moon. It led him to a valley where it bubbled out of rock. Crouching, he tried to scoop it up. But nothing was real and the water leaked through his fingers.

So he dropped back to the small things, touching leaves and spotting insects in the cracks of walls. The air was full of spider threads and sunbeams. Indoors, the dust motes drifted like smoke. But though they were always there, the small things didn't hold him.

Finally, he realised. Everywhere he went the voice of Rima went with him. All day, it whispered in his ear, checking he was there. In the morning, it acted as his guide, marking his way by street and house number. When he reached school, it hid behind a surprised expression. It answered back teachers and laughed at his classmates. In the toilet it told him to hold his breath, in the playground it said *hide*, in the gym it told him *this is not for you*. At home time it crouched behind hedges and sighted rivals with deadly thought rays. As the voice of Rima, he jab-jabbed them where it hurt. And when kid A or B or C appeared, he charged and put them to the sword. Because poetry was his weapon.

"If a poem is concentrated, a closed fist, then a novel is relaxed and expansive, an open hand." *Sylvia Plath*

Hands Up

I

To keep one hand in the air we'd prop it
against walls or use the other as a flying buttress.

The teachers kept us guessing. They were
in the lead, playing safe, taking their time.

"Best man wins!" they called as our faces stiffened
and the wobbles set in.

Our arms were transmitters. Like shirts on
sticks they relayed a thousand SOS messages.

In the struggle to be top, we were divided.
I was a sheep, but goats, of course, win.

If this was our chance to each plead our case
then we all wanted to be chosen.

II

We had to put up our hands to go.

Caught between pride and discomfort,
we were too afraid to speak.

Our insides hurt as we clenched. Using our fingers
as a torque, we held back the flow

and counted.

It all felt damp. We'd a lesson to learn.

When the bell rang it was touch and go.
Everything tingled as the rains came down.

III

Drawing around our hands,
we made them into cave art.

There were ghosts the other side
matching their flesh to ours.

Dipped in ink, our hands became spiders.
Bunched into fists, we waved them at each other.

When we got older we held them out
to meet other hands, and our bodies
flew out of the window.

We were learning to grow.

....

LESLIE TATE

The world seemed quite different when the boy read stories on his own. In stories, things came and went. Like birds or flowers, they were there in the Spring but disappeared later. Poems did that, too. They popped up at night or sometimes in the bath. Afterwards they got lost or didn't seem to matter. With a poem you were never quite sure where it might lead or what it was about. Other people didn't seem to like that. Talking like a poet was difficult, too. The words were strange or went in all directions. Nothing was fixed or certain. With poetry things like deaths and disappearances just happened. They came back as well, but changed utterly. Trying to be a poet was a bit like being in a waking dream.

"I'm your many different selves," said the Poet of the Sky.

"And I'm the stories you never heard," said the Poet of the Wind.

"Imagine life after everything's gone," cried the Angel Poet.

Poetry was hard to hold on to. Like thought it came out of nowhere then quickly passed over. The shapes it took were ephemeral. It arrived and shone and was extinguished. If it existed at all it was an imprint – or imprint of an imprint – a mark of those who went before.

For the boy, just learning a poem was an end in itself. It took him out of himself. While he was reciting it, he lost track of time. Entering its world, he became THE VOICE OF THE BARD. The words had his name on them. As he read them, a still, elevated glow came over him. Nobody could touch him or hurt him anymore. It was a kind of immortality.

And the boy had set his heart on it.

Marking Time

The boy wanted to be remembered.

In the story he was telling he'd fallen from a tree
and been taken to hospital in a coma.

When he woke he was wrapped in linen
and his parents were standing by the bed.

They didn't know what to say.

Being hurt made him untouchable.
Beneath the sheets he'd started to glow.

His recovery took years. He bore it all bravely.
The police arrived with a stretcher
to carry him home.

He had seen and heard things he shouldn't.

During his confinement
he went by the name Delicate.
His blue-striped pyjamas were prison gear.

When he returned to school his body felt
like Liquorice Allsorts inside a tin drum.
There were grenades in his fingers
and a parachute pull-cord connected to his penis.

At any moment
he might burst from the classroom
and break all records on the field.

How would he be remembered?

For pimples and spots,
chewed down fingernails, hair cut short,
letting in goals.

In the eyes of everyone he was ordinary.

3.

My name's Charisma. I'm a nurse and psychic coach.
I look after people with reverse impostor syndrome
(RIS). If you're wondering what that is, just think
of someone small staring into a large mirror. It's not
a condition, more a way of life – one that works for
my clients because their importance is self-evident,
at least to them. I sometimes think of them as people
who occupy a charmed space, but a narrow one, with
just a few devoted admirers. They're like Wagner,
but much more parochial. My job, regardless of talent, is to get them out there so they relate to others.
How do I do that? Well, it's rather like eating choc-
olate: I fill their gaps and cheer them up. And once
inside I get to know them, often better than they
know themselves.

Allow me to give you an example.

Let's suppose you're sitting on a worn canvas chair in an old-fashioned, echoey hall, listening to a talk. On the stage ahead a small man in grey trousers and a holey jumper is speaking. Next to him a pencil-thin woman is following every word. He's telling her about poets – the ones like him and what they said, the readings they've shared, their drinking binges, and the twice-told tales of fishing or trespassing or playing cards together.

But now I'm inside the poet. What I see is a desk and a hand holding a chewed-down biro. The pen's got a life of its own and, when I look closer, I see it's writing a begging letter. My view widens to a desk in a whitewashed room that resembles a monk's cell. I can see, by the poet's shoulder, an angel. I sense they're friends – long-term buddies for life – but the angel's expression is sad. It's the deep, quiet sadness of still water. The same blue sadness as the poet's. I'm seeing right through him.

Out in the room his talk continues. It's down-beat and mumbled, mentioning affairs and scrapes and pants-down moments with the boys – who are elderly like him, and all rather ha-ha-ha-ish. "My collection," he says, expectantly, and the woman hands him a chapbook with a grey cover. Before reading, he flicks between pages. "It's all there," he says, speaking to himself. "Let's find a good one." Raising the book, he clears his throat and a long poem follows, read slowly in a monotone. It ends with a few detached syllables, tailing off into silence. After applause, the woman asks a question and the poet speaks about life and idleness and intoxication. A few more questions and some rambling answers end with the woman recommending the book and the poet declaring himself done.

I return inside. The poet's sadness has deepened. He's awake in the night, pacing his cell. There's slow music in his head. It's a persistent, wave-break of sadness. The song is *Mood Indigo*.

Afterwards I chat to Alice, the pencil-thin woman. Her voice is RP smooth, as if she's reading from an autocue. As she speaks, I noticed her spread hands and appealing smile. "He's a beautiful specimen, isn't he," she says, addressing a spot somewhere behind me.

"And sad," I add.

"Sad?"

I nod.

"You mean what one might call poetically sad?"

"No, the real thing. Depression."

"Thoughts that lie too deep for tears?"

"Deeper. And invisible."

"Really?"

"Even to him."

"But I do so enjoy his company."

I hear what follows, like a recording. A series of clichés, literary ones, including *a real character*, *an original talent* and *one of the founding poets*. But I don't reply. Instead, I've found my way inside again. It's like being behind a screen, watching Alice in a film. I see a figure running. Her, of course, but shadowy, glimpsed in reverse. She's short of breath; struggling, trying to keep up. And the gap between her and the rest of the world is widening.

The poet's sister joins us, introducing herself as Lucretia. "Lou for short," she says. She's large and peepy-eyed with bare pink arms and coiled-up hair. Younger than him, she looks like a cross between a washerwoman and a backing singer. Lou talks about her brother as a youth, smiling as she describes him hiding in the garden. "He was my big play-brother," she says. "It was soooo ludic. Like his poetry." When Alice asks about his youthful compositions, Lucretia answers with a laugh. "He never showed me," she says. "But I sneaked glances. He was Chatterton plus."

Inside Lucretia there's a woman of independent means who's busy revising her books – two imaginary memoires called L1, L2. They feature a Degas-like dancer whose great love appears across a crowded room. L1, L2 are Lucretia's pride and joy. Filed under *pending* at the back of her mind, they are shiny, pocket-sized, and contain hidden messages. They're better than anything her brother has ever written.

I'm about to leave when I'm asked in a deep voice for my views on tonight's poetry. I think I know my questioner. He calls himself Alice's companion and he's carrying a notebook in one hand. To look at him, with his black shirt and hair down to the collar, you'd think he was an 80s musician. But the voice is what gives him away. It's like the poet's voice, given extra depth and resonance. He's a brooding, power-testing type with his own *I'm important* look, and he's aiming his question at me.

My answer's noncommittal. His inquiry has turned our chitchat into an investigation.

"That's clear then," he says. "Not impressed."

I try to hold my ground, but nothing comes out.

"You see, charm – aura, mystique, glamour – none of it works," he adds. "It's all emptiness."

Although he turns away, I've a feeling I'm in the spotlight. He's a kind of all-seeing critic, reading from a private script. His delivery is line by line; around the words and behind the words. His script, of course, is me.

I realise as the silence continues that his name's Marchais. A voice in my head, playing with the letters, tells me why.

4.

"The poet is engaged in something very closely analogous to trying to remember a poem they have forgotten." *Don Paterson*

"The three principles of poetry are soul, song, and formal necessity—the Coleridgean sense of formal necessity that the poem should contain within itself the reason why it is thus and not otherwise." *Derek Mahon*

Nightingale

These repeat-notes with step-change and
chorus, heard through glass,
tunester in a wall spot,
leaf-fringed, by blocks,
piped up from the roadside,
might be a recording

or snatches from a poem, sounding in the head.

Old notes in darkness,
going out from a garden
led by a cellist and broadcast on the Beeb★.

Here, tuned in to shadow, by traffic,
love bird and instrument guesting unnoticed,
plays ad lib, impro and riff.

And the sudden change in set, up sticks
with listeners from chamber to outdoors,
to mid-May live,
as the on-air, breath-held woman
stirs dark sounds into wood
to coax up the birds.

Or poet in close-up, caught speaking low,
working the changes on a near-death experience.

Deliberate, we are there.
Still hear the dream-songs
in odd spots, build-ups, crossings
and stop-offs behind walls.
Or here, taking up position,
all ears at the window,
for lead-break, DJ, night bird, heart throb
(that song again, that song again)
encore and finale
to cut across the dark.

And not be interrupted.

★ On May 19, 1924, the Savoy Orphean BBC radio concert was interrupted to go to the garden of virtuoso cellist Beatrice Harrison where she was heard playing, accompanied by local nightingales. The performance was so popular it was repeated annually until 1936.

Some poems are like paper darts. They fit into a hand and balance on air. Their folds are exact. They generate lift and can survive crash landings. Everything about them is precisely calculated. Step inside their bodies and they are larger than life. They are more than the sum of their parts.

"Poetry is the art of saying things once." *Don Paterson*

Lacewing

Green and inverted
on a white-textured ceiling
you have mailed yourself
to arrive in outline
like an X-marks-the-spot,
join-up-the-dots,
finepoint,
narrowtip,
throwback image
taken from a film.

With your folded paper wings
and thinned-down flesh
you're up there keeping still,
a cloudscape pointer
lodged against plaster,
hooked and veined like a fish in the sky.

Your ceremonials begin.
Forward and back,
matching moves,
in step and out
your turn – no your turn – no-no, afteryou
when I hold up paper to slide you out.

Using a jam jar I carry you around,

rim-perched and elevated,
on a big dipper ride
to the exit window
where it seems you're paused,
looking out, top of the programme.

To unsaddle
you gently
edge-tipped, then touching,
takes surprise and finesse.

Suddenly, Disney-ish,
star-wishing life unfolds into flags.
Map lines and coordinates
open over white.
Needle-dancing you drop,
then pick up and rise
like a deus ex machina.

On the face of it, everything I write is auto-fiction. Even if it's third-person I can reference some of it to my life. I seem to need some kind of realia to set me going – which can be a remembered phrase or an image from the past. That means, although I try to write outside my experience I find, in the end, only the personal does it.

But this reliance on experience makes me feel at times that my imagination is limited. Of the two types of writer, adapters and fantasists, I'm with the former. Even my commentaries are poetic and personal. I'm not the sort of author who reads about something in the newspapers and turns it into story or an article.

As a writer, I find myself blending together 'me' and 'them'. I call it the super-personal. As I write through my characters, I'm looking for turns of phrase that point towards the generic and the wider context.

Perhaps all writing is a coming-of-age story. It's certainly a trial-and-error thing. In the process of writing and promoting our work we may find ourselves in a room on our own or bigging ourselves up in a bargain basement. Some authors learn the 'rules', others go it alone, many give up. If the main myth of our times is the rise and fall of the *wunderkind*, then we're all individualists on mission impossible. For me, to record that journey may be risky and the mindset complex but what counts is the person we become – and the qualities it brings to a book.

1.

I present an internet radio show where I interview local guests and play their musical choices. It's a 24/7 station, going out from a studio in a rundown building next to flats at the top of a hill. To enter the studio, I type in codes on a keypad and switch off an alarm, then cross a large room to a doorway in the corner. The studio's in there, sealed behind glass like a space capsule. Inside its white-walled box there are computers, monitors, control boards with lights and sliders, photos of presenters, and three oval-shaped mics hung like lightbulbs from metal arms.

The studio door usually stands open, so sometimes the broadcast picks up ghostly noises from the next-door dance class, or chatter from the big room. It's a sign of the radio station's openness. It's also the only way to stop the studio overheating.

Today, as usual, I arrive early. The big room feels like an entrance hall. It's a meeting place for techies, creatives, chatterers and people on a mission. But this evening it's quiet except for a trickle of sound issuing from the studio. I put down my bag then poke around with a USB behind a computer. I'm rehearsing the interview in my mind. Glancing at my watch, I go to the studio and check the main screen. Reading its blue and pink bars, I see there's an overrun, but I'm nervous of correcting it. Is it OK to delete? Do I know what I'm doing? And if I bin some tracks, can I restore them? Finally I do delete, one track at a time. A voice inside me says it's fine, but another voice is telling me I've blundered.

The doubt continues when I return to the big room to prepare my show. Sitting at the computer, I work my way through a succession of searches, playbacks, conversions, numbered carts and edits, using headphones occasionally to monitor my work. When I've finished, even though I've got half an hour to go, I'm unsettled. There's a fear that one click too many or a wrong command might end up in silence.

I did silence my show once. I was trying out effects with sliders. It was the first time and I forgot about the voice mics. The music faded and I launched into what I thought was a jolly-jolly announcement. Switching to my guest I continued chatting without realising no one could hear us.

But today my guest is a musician, and that's comforting because J has recorded several albums, so he understands radio. I do know he'll have to tune up and then hit the note, which makes his job harder than mine. With that comes a thought: maybe he'll want sound that's super-high quality? For a second I'm reminded of my weekly comedown after the show. But everything changes as he walks in.

J's lean and chiselled, slightly bearded, young and rugged - a perfect indie rocker – and surprisingly diffident. But get past that and he's deep, as I soon discover. Speaking *sotto voce*, he says hello and I show him to the studio, asking about his music. After tuning up and a mic check, we talk about the interview. There's a gentleness about him and a hint of sadness. It's as if he's searching for a lost song. Maybe he's been unlucky in love or he's on a long journey, there's a hidden story that makes him who he is.

Our on-air session goes quickly. We're both performers, so we fill up every moment with words, songs, guitar riffs and stories. It's unscripted and surprising. There's a polished, high-energy power to J's music – he's a singer/guitarist with a big band – but when he stops playing he reverts to his private self.

"I have these moments… Minor key stuff. You might call them downs."

My reply is a prompt. "Downs? You mean something like The Bends, Radiohead?"

J's answer begins slowly, like a filler, then changes tempo. "The truth is, yes. Or sort of yes. It's more like doubts, really. I've always had anxiety. It's the thought that at any moment things might fall apart. And the doubt itself can bring on just the thing you don't want. It's about being alone – maybe thinking too much – counting all the losses."

"So how does that work when you go on stage?"

"Oh, performing clears it. That's when I get to let go. Every gig's brilliant."

"So, don't think about it, just do it, eh? That's a quote, by the way. Pink Fairies."

"Yes, I get that…" Again, his voice slows, then switches up: "But I'd also like to say that anxiety has its uses."

"It does? Can you explain?"

"Well, all my songs are about it, one way or the other. It's a drive. Because when I get worried, I sing about it. I think I'm filling a hole, heart on a sleeve, whatever. My music's full of it."

I nod and thank him. I say it's good for the listeners to know. I find myself using words like *where it comes from* and *making it happen* as I ask him to play again. Not because we need to fill up time but because what he's just said is one of those special, off-the-scale moments: a radio first. It stays with me as he tunes up and I joke about how musicians fuss. It accompanies his performance and my applause at the end and remains in the background as I thank him and wrap up the show.

When we're off air, I check that he's happy with how it went.

"Happy," he says.

"The stuff about anxiety – that's OK?"

He nods. As I watch him pack up his guitar, I feel something flattening inside.

"Great show," I say as I set the alarm and usher him out.

We part in a bare concrete space beneath a broken street lamp. Behind us the radio block is lit from inside. I know that light. It's that special place where the voice in the air speaks and anything can happen. I know it from inside, like a child sheltering in a cave. It's a world on its own full of dreams and special effects. Though in fact, what I can see is the glow of the alarm through holed curtains.

"Dark out here," I say.

"But the show goes on," he says, pointing to the block.

My last glimpse as I drive off is a man on a motorbike with a guitar strapped to his back. On the way home I listen to the radio. The song I hear is Joy Division, "Transmission".

....

I'm walking with Sue Hampton along a lane at the edge of our town recording my radio show on a phone.

We're talking about the greenery, the spring flowers, and reading from our joint book. It's an easy, relaxed walk, but keeping up a commentary is an effort. So, my voice as it takes on the rhythm of our feet, sounds unsteady, and because I've a phone in one hand and a book in the other, turning the pages is a fiddle. Also, there's no script or autocue, and each passing car drowns out our voices. But most of all, this show is live; one take only.

But why on a phone? Mainly because we're locked down, so I have to email my shows to the station manager to put them in the playout. And because I'm not a techie, an app on a phone's the best I can do.

Of course, I'm aware that my phone can play tricks – ads break in; it can suddenly lose volume or whoosh in the wind. But today all goes well. The sun is shining, the trees are budding and we've left the houses behind. As we pass beneath a main road, we're comparing working on a story to walking in the woods. There's a randomness about both, we say, but there are choices as well. We mention *viewpoint* and *compositional*. For us, a novel is a testbed for ideas but the woods are real.

The trees are now 300 yards away and we're filling in radio time until we get there. Reaching a kissing gate, we enter and the mood changes.

Inside is half sun, half shade. I ask Sue to talk and she describes the leaves on the ground, saying they're brown and grey, sometimes black around the edges, and pitted by rain. She goes on to describe the moss, the ivy and the new grass shoots, naming the evergreens behind as holly, laurel and pine. As she talks, I'm thinking of a phrase adapted from an artist I know. It's a fantasy, but one that keeps returning. The phrase is *slow radio*, where the airwaves fill up with something that develops at its own pace, without pressure.

I know my idea isn't practical, but it makes me think about radio and the need to say something. "Oh yes, I'm still here," the DJ says, loudly, to stop people switching off. Because silence, like a vacuum, has to be avoided.

But what's *slow radio*, you ask? What does it sound like and does it have an audience?

For it to work, it requires concentration, like chess, or an ear pressed against a party wall between houses. And, as it's hush-hush, it takes time to make sense. So the broadcast comes and goes; it's a kind of night-music where the audience follow clues while hearing sounds in the distance.

We keep up the talk. We compare walking in the woods to the concentrated power of stories. There are birdcalls and footfalls between our words. The trees are in leaf and the sun strikes the path. If this is slow radio, it's *pianissimo*. A place where the mind takes over and stillness leads. It's step-by-step and subliminal.

When we reach the middle of the woods we chat about endings. Nowadays nothing's cut and dried, we say, so the last page is more of a rest stop than a reveal. To wrap up, we mention side tracks, hidden paths and the road not taken. Then Sue tells the listeners about forest bathing, I say something about *slow radio*, and we sign off together.

……………………………..

Ok, this is Leslie Tate (Note To Self (NTS): don't use *OK*) on Radio R with another show just for you (NTS: *another* is wrong, too downbeat/boring).

And this evening I'm going to take you on a really amazing walk (CUT *really amazing* IT'S CLICHÉ!) on the canal towpath near where I live, recorded on my phone. (Pause, gathering breath, trying to find words…)

Oh shit. Delete that. Start again.

Good evening this is Radio R with Leslie Tate for your evening entertainment (Stop! Don't use EVE-NING twice.)

That's a mess. Avoid repetition – it's the author in me. Start again.

Hi there, Leslie Tate of Radio R bringing you music and talk; talk and music. Now hold on there you lovely listeners while I take you on a walk along the canal towpath (but what about music? Will they stay listening?), beginning at…

(NTS: Now off… Walk that walk – as practised – talk that talk. The mind's on the move; it just happens. The voice is you.)

At this point, listeners, we're coming up to some waterbirds. You can probably hear them honking; it's a gaggle of geese close to the path. They're all over the grass. And uh-oh, one of them has chicks – and, yes, she's hissing. You may be able to hear the hissing on this phone. She's angry – doing that lunging thing with her neck. So I'm keeping my distance. The trouble is I'm pretty scared, but I'm doing my best not to show it in case that provokes her. Anyway, I'm just about past her and she's still hissing but not lunging any more… And now we're going under a bridge and you can hear it echoing.

(Talking out of breath. Unsmooth presenter. Cartoon image of unfit runner. You have to laugh.)

And this is the turning point where the canal widens and opens out. It's the place where the narrow boats used to turn. A bit like those old-fashioned turntables for trains. Funnily enough it's close to the railway station, just over there. Of course, all the main routes run along the valley bottom. This is the way through the hills for road, rail and canal. And the castle's here as well, just behind the railway embankment. It's broken down now, but it used to be one of the most important castles outside London…

(Remembering history at school. Soooooo boring. Got to say something different. But are there are any listeners?)

And now we've arrived at a garden. It's a riot of colour. Daffodils, yellow, of course. Their real name is narcissi, though people tend to use that name for the smaller papery ones that smell. In fact they all smell. To the ancient Greeks they didn't just smell, they stank, which made them part of the underworld. And next to them I can see hellebores – they're the pale flowers with their heads down – and crocuses. It's very seasonal but early, with lots of plants flowering all at the same time. That's because of climate change...

(Important to get that in. But keep it short. coming to an end. Sign off soon.)

We're at our last bridge now and the end of our walk. So if you want to enjoy anything I've talked about, just get outdoors if you can, when you can. And if you can't go out right now, save it for another day. It's something to celebrate, a lucky dip thing, and a great time of year with all the flowers popping up. This is Leslie Tate of Radio R on the canal signing off...

(Click that button. Shaky now. One take, never perfect. Same voice – maybe tiring? But only human. A kind of authorship.)

....

I'm learning how to develop my radio-self. I'm practising talking fast, trotting out thoughts, asides, reminders and off-the-cuff remarks. It's a version or edit of who I am. And to do it, I take in the music so I'm in the mood, imagining myself centre stage. But even then, sometimes I flow, sometimes I hesitate, and sometimes get stuck. And when that happens, I know it.

So here's my cautionary tale.

At the age of six, Polly appeared on stage, playing a child without a name. She made the part her own.

As the youngest in the cast, she was supposed to lie on stage in a yellow tent, sleeping. But when the boys began to sing, she got up and started an arms-in the-air, side-to-side dance. It surprised the boys, who forgot their words until Polly beckoned them to her and led them, singing, round the stage. But this time the words were crazy, single-syllable grunts and high squeaks. She was in the spotlight, a child-whizz who waved her arms and opened her mouth and suddenly (although, surely, it was a dream) Polly grew wings and took off – but then the lights darkened and she began to fall. She was a feather in a wind, rocking side to side, or a moth in darkness. And as she fell, the voices rose to meet her. They were the boys as a pre-dawn chorus and, also, the audience cheering. Nobody saw as she dropped backstage and entered the tent. And then she was alone. When the lights went up, she heard a voice calling, but though she shaped her mouth, nothing came out. It was then that she heard it. As the boys and the audience began to leave, she started to cry. The child she'd played was called Lost.

After the Crash

All the radio stations in the world began to play.

At the Earth's last gig,
they were the backing tracks
and studio edits of long-forgotten hits
exiting the machine.

They spread like water, finding ways in
through locked back doors
and boarded-up windows.

Their jingles and adverts echoed back
from the choir stalls and pulpits
of deserted churches.

Heard in the head they were the deep base notes
of storms out to sea and icebergs breaking up.

In a moment of truth
they cut to force 10 lead breaks
and wild cries of rage and loss
that bounced off buildings
in a wall of sound,

then hushed themselves to
fingerpicking riffs
and all-night moves with close-mike vocals

that retell the story
of Earth-loss, exile and breakdown
and love holding out

while a bloodbath was happening.

2.

In the dream I've just had, the radio station has been reduced to a single screen mounted on a desk in an empty classroom. The screen works, but there's something slightly odd about how it looks. Although it's fixed on wood, the picture keeps rocking about, as if it's at sea. Looked at closely, it's dark around the edges. I've an unsettled feeling of groping for an exit with people pushing past. There's a voice in my head, telling me my show is due. It's my announcer voice – smooth and joined-up and calmly jolly. It's a cover, of course, because my show's not ready, or to be exact, the songs are ready but my mouse won't work. I tell myself to stay calm as I roll it around, then tap it on the mat. When the arrow appears, I seek out the tabs at the top of the screen, only to find they're jammed. I'm on edge now, wishing I'd never started this. I press a few keys – hard – try out various stops, fiddle and jab, but nothing seems to work. I'm misting over, time's up, and I go around in circles, trying the same clicks again and again. It's a closed loop, a no-go area, a blockage.

So what's this all about? And why does it keep coming back?

84

It's a compilation dream, running together the heavy control tactics of a lifetime's teaching and the panic induced by misbehaving technical devices.

But why's it always about performing? The answer, I think, is another story. Or two stories in one.

I remember a university seminar where we took turns presenting a book. I chose *Sartor Resartus* by Carlyle and began reading around my subject. I kept on reading and taking notes as the deadline approached, ending with 20 pages of disorganised scrawl. The book's thickness and grandiose style seemed to require it. I was living the spirit of Carlyle's afflatus, and that put me on a par with him.

On seminar day I sat down at the end of a long table and began sorting my papers. I kept rearranging them, but whatever I did I couldn't find a thread to take me through. The lecturer was staring at me and saying my name, but still I couldn't get my papers in order. I had a sense that the room had emptied out and nothing really mattered. At the same time my head was hot and my legs were shaking. In the end, when the lecturer called time, I launched in extempore.

What followed was a halting, incoherent, stop-go mumble – breaking out into sudden rants – then tailing off to an appeal, and silence. It reminded me of my performance in the mock-general election at school where I'd been the Communist Party candidate. When my turn came at the hustings, I was booed offstage.

So the performance is a testing ground. In my case, I deliberately went for impossible tasks – or I made them as difficult as I could. Because behind these examples is pride and self-obsession. Trying to prove myself, against the odds. Going places where others wouldn't go.

But the dream's more about survival. It's a game of chance where we face everything that bad luck can throw at us. Because once it's out there it loses its power. And it points to something bigger than ourselves.

Because behind every performer is the appeaser, the exorcist and the God.

3.

My name's Tagalong. I'm *not a bot* and my friend's a stand-up comedian. I've known him all my life. He's small, slight, cheery-eyed, spotty all over (let's say I've seen him in the shower) and young – although in fact he's forty-ish, jobless and sponging off his mother. She calls him Toots, though his real name's Trevor, which he says with a long E and a round-mouth O, laughing like a toff, then TREV when challenged by a heckler with *who do you think you are*? Trev the trucker and Trev the brickie, he says, for chewing in your mouth. But then he's baby-face again, all apologies and talking about his fuck ups. He calls it his anti-comedy, where you don't quite know if he's acting the lad or really messing up. Sometimes I think he's not quite sure himself. He's like one of those old-fashioned clocks with figures on the hour popping out – the one that appears is usually a surprise.

"Comedy's an attitude," he says.

"Bad?" I ask.

He shakes his head.

"Then what?"

"It's a way of being serious. Saying stuff."

"You mean said the actress to the bishop – that kind of thing?"

"Pretty much. The naked truth."

"But you set out to shock, yeah?"

"Yes indeedy. Throw in a few rocks. Keeps 'em awake."

"Which means it's a wind-up?"

"Or *if you're thinking what I'm thinking*."

"So it's really about pushing buttons?"

"Yup. And it can hide depression."

That's my Trev for you. To look at him you'd think, "He's a fun guy." When he does a 10 or a 20, it's as if you're inside his mouth. Or he's a cat burglar, climbing inside your head. Then he takes a walk round the room, rambles a bit, but just as you're getting into what he's saying, swerves into something off-piste. Just watch his body language – it's all there. He stares too much, then switches expression like a kid in headlights. Sometimes he goes deadpan or pauses too long between words and you wonder what coming next. There's a hidden nod, a wink and a trapdoor opening. Trev's got you guessing.

You want to know more about his depression? That's another question. Trev tells it like this: "If you're all day standing in the corner it gets to a point where you either wet your pants or go up in smoke.

That was me as a kid. Most of the time I was in disguise. I had this crowd of imaginary people trying to get out. You wouldn't have known it, though. I kept everything low. Very, very, low. In company, my mouth was in my boots. It's what people mean when they say 'he wanted the floor to swallow him up'."

When I ask him where his jokes come from, he says this: "It's like I've got this CCTV trained on myself. There's no let up. I'm watching the bad stuff and turning it into funnies, or shoutouts."

Trevor's old-fashioned. He likes double-decker buses, red ones with adverts for cocoa on the side, and plasticine strips he shapes into animals. He rubs his tummy, pats his head and sings *Green Grow the Rushes O*, watching himself in a shop window. "Yum, yum," he says as he chews on jelly babies. When it comes to clothes, he's into flares and sparkly waistcoats. When he's in the mood he talks like David Niven, but swearily, as if he was impersonating the shadow side. Even then, he throws in apologies and fluffs his lines, so you can't tell whether he's doing it for effect or losing the plot.

In the end, Trevor picks you up, gets you interested, then drops you in it. He's a teaser, a both-ways-facer, one foot on land, one on sea. He's the card you play when you want to outfox your opponents. He's in it, he says, for the practical stuff – by which he means walking under ladders, stepping in shit and joshing with followers like me.

"Lots of take-off, and up yours," he says, "and keep it OUCH!"

What he means is comedy can burn your fingers.

"Sounding the alarm," I say, nodding.

"Burning bridges," he replies.

"Hot potatoes," I call.

"Scorched earth," he says.

"Yeah. Tonight we're on fire," I tell the audience. Then I look around.

"Did I just say that?" I ask.

"Hey, who's on the bill tonight?" demands a heckler.

"Hello!" I call back.

You guessed it. Trevor's me.

....

Which doesn't mean I'm REALLY him or he's me. Because I've got my own voice too. I'm the long-faced man who cuts himself with a razor and drips blood on the carpet as he shuffles to the bedroom looking for a plaster. When I get there, it takes me a while to real-ise that I'm in the nudie. So I put on a gown covered with skeleton pics and pull faces in the mirror. I'm the undertaker man who comes on stage to a Nick Cave track and dances the Paso Doble. Except the only per-son frightened is me. I'm the kid in the corner shut-ting my eyes pretending that no one can see me. If they laugh it's because I'm laughable.

And now – rat-a-tat-tat– for the squirm-making stuff.

When I'm in a rush I've been known to trip over my own feet. Trip over your own feet, you say, how on earth…? Well, I do. It's possible. It's a kind of training for playing the fool. Not the wise fool type and not accidentally-on-purpose but the slapstick clown. It's something I do to dodge the bullets. I once had a friend who told me that the best defence is to take the piss out of yourself. It makes people drop their guard. Mess-upery, I call it. You can imagine me flat out on stage waving my legs like a beetle on its back. I'm the striker who overruns the ball and ends up diving into mud. It's quite an art, chucking yourself in the air to land nose-against-the-deck. It's a great audience participation gag – and that's when I get them to count. One-two-three and I sit up and fall back like a KO-ed boxer. It's up and down, Grand Old Duke of York, before clambering onto a chair then tripping over again. And I do it in slowmo, like a silent movie extra. I'm drunk or mad – which in a way I am. Because I'm a natural – the boy in the bath with two rubber ducks, that's me. And I cry a lot. But behind my peek-a-boo image I've got my eye on you. Yes, really. I'm stone cold and serious, and nothing escapes me. I'm a kind of psycho-in-hiding. Crocodile tears and fake foolery. And yes, you know what happens with stage-types. The shadow dances differently.

Now who's joking?

4.

'Poetry is a cage with an animal inside… it has a wild longing for clarity.' *Derek Mahon*

Last Songs

The woodpeckers fill the forest
with trills and appoggiatura.

Again and again, they practise their alarms.
Can you feel the Earth shake? they ask.

and the bare wood runs:
live-wood, wet-wood, soft-wood,
moss-wood that pops up shows.

The woodpeckers know what's coming. It's a
dying fall.

Knock knock, they say
as they dodge behind trunks.

as the old-wood bends,
air-swells and thickens, puts itself around.

The woodpeckers play their tune.
It's a single, rhythmic, on-all-sides signature
that drills down to a stop.

Behind it they're counting.
1-2-3-4 this is how we're gonna go.

and the air flows in through stripped-down
passageways, turns about and about,
to go to earth quietly.

The woodpeckers keep busy.
Hear our Last Songs, they say,
finding their entries
through wood-pulse and hush
to hit on flesh.

as woodearth, soft-blown,
peaking and unfolding pipes up stems.

Tail-braced, crouching, clinging like flies,
the woodpeckers call time.

5.

"A poem begins in delight and ends in wisdom."
                    Robert Frost

Field Daisies

I

Are small postage
or cards on the table.

Teaspoons, sugar cubes,
mirrors to the sun.

Count them as stars
fallen on cloth,

particles, dust motes,
eye drops,
heads on coins.

II

Underheel, they slide away.
Play ready or not.
Take over on the lawn
to populate the garden
in an open, free and easy,
cheerful, knees and elbow jostle.
A you-me-and-the-dog
where they crowd, rub shoulders,
dig deep and scratch
(or strong, play four-square and squat

to knock heads together).

III

Dice throws. Counters.
Colour and shape with minor variations.
Strains that meet
to give and offer thoughts,
best bits, mood scraps
and flavours run together.

Crumbs of wisdom.

The slow way is to put it in writing. Word by word – crafted, examined, looked up in the dictionary and recast again and again. It's a double deck of cards, shuffled and dealt out in a game of patience – one that never ends. And behind the writing there's a guessing game, a back-and-forth shift, attempting to find a way. If it's in writing, then it has to be perfect.

BUT when you speak, you're in the hotseat. At the turn of a switch, it's live and there you are! There's presence and connection. The voice leads, pausing and repeating and putting in 'you knows' and 'sort ofs', and sometimes struggling for a word or a placename. Then, without warning, it all comes out in a rush.

Writing's more accurate, of course – quotes and looking up facts, checking for meanings and weeding out redundancies – but what makes a book is the coming together of disciplined telling and random asides. It's the oral-in-the-written, the trained voice on-air, the formal and the casual. All that, and the edit, brings the book to life. The trick is in the mix.

1.

I'm afraid of the dark. It's the child in me who imagines trolls under beds and ogres behind doors. That child is close to the edge, so I can still sense attackers nearby and ghosts round corners. It's all part of the shadowy figures on my tail and the bad thoughts in my head. I'm the boy alone in a gallery tiptoeing past Victorian portraits with eyes that follow him.

My phobia means I don't understand horror. Its crude hammer blows both confuse and alarm me. Why self-harm that way? And why look at a picture that makes you want to throw up, or play nightmare games that overwhelm you? It seems so self-indulgent. I also don't understand taking pleasure in dark endings or psychotic characters or having Halloween 'fun'. It's a kind of look-at-me gesture that seems anti-life.

In analysing phobia, Freud diagnosed Separation Anxiety Disorder – as in the story of children lost in the woods – where life can take on any shape and we can't tell what might happen next. It's fear of self, the dark inside, and being cast out. It makes us aware of our dependency at every breathing moment. It's a memento mori.

Visit

My mother's in the kitchen as we knock
and enter. We're expected.
Except for the kisses and silk-grey hairdo,
she's unchanged. Her dewlap cheeks are warm.
After passing through health checks,
teabag squeezings and the week in headlines,
we occupy the lounge.

Inviting us to sit, she hunts out coasters.
Our talk begins again. Inside its structure
– tape loop or formula – I'm invisible,
standing at the window,
observing the small boy with shadow self
and hideouts, surrounded by branches
on the wrong side of the shed.

Or jumpy on the beach,
crowding the camera in shorts and sandals
with background wheel and dog.

She's present tense.
There are briefings, shopping trips, reminders,
exchanges with my partner and updates
on sale price and improvements for the house.

I nod and question, while the picture widens
to out-of-focus snaps on sunlit lawns,
hands on glasses and cars driving off
and the all-white faces when the shutter sticks.

My first, while cornering, legs together
pressed on leather, ridge-marked to a rash.
Backseat in the Austin, I knew I was stuck;
one false move and the flesh might tear.
Hitting a pothole, the camera flashed
on a door swung back, air scooped out
and darkness spinning like vinyl.

Everything stopped
with the talk-shouts that followed.

Or remained in outline, a moment in waiting,
imagined often when trying not to look.

What the eye doesn't see.

Next in the glare, running the lawn,
bared to a grin, with trunks and mud splats
in a blown-up pool. And the dream-shots later
of shoulders peeling in low-cut suntops,
eyeing the wasps crawling through jam.

Then off-cuts held up: the frost-palms and ferns
caked on glass, the black brass weights
held in the balance by Fairy-soft hands,

the sewing attachments tangled in a drawer,
the skin flaps, nail splits
and door-trapped fingers.

Don't look now.

Finally in the dark: the slide round the corner
and catch in the breath as the boy jumps sleep
to stand peering out
through flesh-wrapped curtains
dream-lost and floaty in deep cold water.

And now we're standing, talking by the door.
There are items to pick up, smiles and promises,
timings, and next week's visit.

When we leave, it's late.
On our journey home, the headlights cut a line.
We follow back the thread.
Inside the beam, bordered by darkness,
the road runs forward.
Outside that, we're surrounded
by things we can't see.

What Jamie Saw

2.

Jamie believed that when he died his life would begin again. Like Big Ben or the living room clock the hands would circle round while he wasn't watching – or maybe they ran backwards? Somehow things did that behind his back. Like *The Sorcerer's Apprentice* they jiggled and danced to unheard tunes then jumped to attention when his parents appeared. In the mirror, too, there were dreams in reverse. Backside-first and inside-out, as if he was reconstructing a crime or walking blindfold through someone else's house.

As far as his break-ins went, he didn't know whether they really happened. In his head he shadowed the girl four doors down, slipping in unseen and following her to the kitchen. Hidden beneath the table he heard everything.

"Amanda dear," her mother called, opening the back door, "I'd like you to walk for me."

Although she didn't react, Jamie could see the girl was listening. Her eyes were round and her cheeks were pink.

"Chin up, back straight," called her mother as they left the house. "You have to be a lady."

Staring from the doorway, Jamie saw Amanda stepping up and down the path.

"Deportment," cried her mother. "Keeping frame."

Head in the air, Amanda did her turns. When she cat-walked forward it was toe-first. Her returns were more upright – but when she spun on her heel something opened like a flower in the sun.

"Lawn dear, and position"

Moving into place, Amanda stood ready. Her expression was dreamy and her hair was in her eyes.

"Now, DANCE."

Amanda stepped forward. When she moved, she was herself; when she stopped, she was a cat. It was almost as if she was stalking her own shadow. To Jamie it felt as if she'd grown up in front of him.

If he died now, he'd come back as Amanda.

Another time, unknown to his parents, he spied on the boys by the garages. They were older than him. Their hands were restless and their faces hard. He was glad they couldn't see him.

"Smoke?" said Keith their leader, though it wasn't really a question. The cigarette in his hand was for passing round, in silence. Smoking was a serious job.

"Smoke more," said Andy, his deputy, as he chain-lit another ciggie and passed it the other way.

When both cigarettes reached a boy called Toby, he double-puffed, then raised them like drumsticks. "Look!" he cried as smoke drifted over their heads. As he passed them on, his hands were shaking.

Two more boys took turns. One held his breath while tapping off the seconds with his foot. Gradually, his face tightened and his shoulders squared until the pain took over, and he began to cough.

The other boy opened his mouth in a rough O and blew out a smoke ring.

Nobody noticed the gap where Jamie sat. The cigarettes passed through him like X-rays. He felt them burning – a spark, first on, then off. They hurt.

If he died holding a cigarette, he'd be toast.

When Jamie went to the cinema, he was in the dark. Sitting between parents, it felt like church. They'd come for his birthday. To eat ice cream and popcorn and look smart and set an example. His hair was slicked back like his dad's. The shoes he wore were leather and tight like his mum's. Now they were seated, his dad was breathing hard and pulling at his tie. His mum had smell on and had permed her hair. Jamie was on best behaviour.

They'd come here to guard him. He was their responsibility. They wanted him to enjoy himself, but going out was a business and the cinema had to be paid for. It could all backfire. But Jamie had kept on asking. He'd pleaded and promised and reminded. And once he knew they had tickets, he'd been extra good. Now he'd got here, Jamie was saying thank you to God.

The film was *20,000 Leagues Under the Sea*. When the orchestra struck up the sea closed in. It was grey-green and wavy and filled the hall. Jamie remembered being at an aquarium. At the sound of a horn, the Nautilus appeared. It was fish-like and spikey with a window as an eye. The ramrod on the front could saw through metal. Its undersea movement was drum-like and menacing. During the first battle it homed in on a gunship and rammed it. Sparks flew and a trumpet blared. Afterwards it went missing. Steered by Nemo, it cruised past reefs and rose in sight of land. When it broke the surface, it spouted like a whale.

In his seat, Jamie dug in. As Ned he speared the squid and threw out bottles asking for help. As Arronax he was clever, as Nemo he was mad. And when the Nautilus hit a rock and the cymbals clashed, he watched Nemo drown. Seeing his face at the porthole was unbearable. His hero had gone and the loss left him empty. A bell tolled slowly as the credits ran. When the lights went up Jamie's eyes were red and his face all puffy.

When his parents saw him, they didn't understand. This couldn't be him. First they wiped his face, then told him to stop. It was only a film.

If he came back as Nemo he'd be the sacrificial lamb.

The old one-two

I

Class 5C were playing in the rain.
As they kicked and went down,
they shouted, calling it a dirty match.

Someone got stomped on.
With the wind against them
they threw up their arms and yelled PENALTY.

Being 5C they were famous.

So who were their heroes
and what did they stand for?

As squaddies they were on target.
As escaped POWs they hit the ground running.
As the team out of hell they took route one.

Between runs they held their sides and scowled.

What did they say, splashing through mud?
Ref. Replay. Wrong. Fix. Offside. Foul. Unfair.
Mostly, they just floundered.

At half time, changing ends,
they dragged their feet as if they'd been wounded.

The rain had filled their boots.

And their names?

Baggy, Messy, Clever Clogs, Chop Chop,
Fidget, Burper, Dodger, Pimple,
Big Foot, Fixer and Lout.

II

All that summer the boy at the back
had dreamed of being in charge.

He'd be the cannonball striker who scored
with a high-dive backflip somersault.

Later he blocked all shots
by turning his body into a No Entry sign.

He was the comeback kid
who wore the armband as bully repellent.

Turned Pied Piper,
he drew off the other side's defenders.

And when he launched his tackles
he became the spade that dug up gold.

Afterwards, his legend lived on.
Nicknamed *Long Shot,* he was in the air

nodding in the equaliser when the ground
came up and hit him.

He missed. Nobody cheered.

As for class 5C: when the final whistle blew
they quick-marched him to the changing rooms
where they all piled in with penalties
while grinning madly
as if their lives depended on it.

3.

Sometimes when I write, I'm surprised by what comes out. It can be awkward. Then again, it can be educational. What I write is both real and made-up – let's call it life-fiction – which means I'm digging into memory to find out who I am, or what I did. There are questions and answers that don't add up – mainly about what I saw and what I missed. So this is a confessional and I'm giving witness against myself.

To begin with the facts. I'm 75, white, male and a retired teacher. My career started in a 12-form entry London comprehensive. I can picture the building: flat-roofed, two-storey with red and white panels, dirty windows and holes kicked in walls. Built in two squares it had a corridor running round the building that provided a walkway for pupils dodging lessons. And the width of the corridor meant that they could promenade in gangs.

The class I was given was bottom stream and nearly all male. As ROSLA kids, they acted as if they were political prisoners. So they walked the corridor pretending not to notice the lessons had started. I'd stand at my classroom door steward-like, waving them in, but they kept going, for anything up to 20 minutes. Even then, a double lesson would seem like a lifetime sentence.

Once in, they sprawled across chairs and wrote on desks or complained they were bored or argued about football. I'd been warned, so I read them bad-boy stories, but books weren't their thing, they said, and when I tried to read on, they drowned me out with shouty interruptions.

The shoutiest was Harry, who was a fidget, the wildest was Jane, the skin-girl, but the sharpest was Carl, who questioned everything.

"Why d'you bother?" he asked, staring at me.

"You know everything?" he added, shaking his head.

"These teachers – a joke," he said, turning to the others. He was pulling rank, and making sure I knew it.

Of course I was shaken, although I tried not to show it. I'd intended to teach them in a nice, bright, even-handed way but already I'd sensed that wasn't on. In fact, the school was a kind of enforced timeout where rumours circulated, bad things happened and all that mattered was survival. In my mind I heard phrases like *shape up*, *learn the score* and *get used to it*. So, to help me get through, I adopted a lie.

The lie was a trick I played on myself. A sleight of hand where I was the victim, allowing me to ignore what was really happening. And as part of that lie, I told myself that teaching – the good sort I believed in – didn't do anything. So I ditched the talk and gave them titles, telling them if they wrote half a page they could play cards.

At first they didn't believe me. Teachers were strange and said weird things. And in any case, they didn't trust anyone. But when Carl said quietly he'd do it, the others joined in. From then on, my classroom became a playground. The card game, followed by dominos and then jacks, kept them busy. And when they wrote, although it wasn't much, their efforts were enough, and by the end of the year they were all awarded grades. All except Carl, who had stopped coming. At the time I didn't ask why, but I wasn't sorry. I knew he was clever, but he'd asked tricky questions and got under my skin. In any case, I wanted to pass my probation – which I did by default, as the teacher shortage meant I wasn't observed.

So what had I missed?

It was years later when I met Carl on the street that I finally understood. He'd greeted me by name, questioned the card games, then told me his story. It just came out, like one of those catchup conversations that happen at parties. But as he talked I noticed how watchful he'd become. "We defend ourselves," he said, glaring at some police gathering on a corner.

"Babylon," he said, pointing to their van.

The officers were closing in on two young women. Both were black. When an officer pulled out handcuffs, Carl stepped forward.

"Leave-leave. Leave be. These're sisters," he called, blocking with his body. He continued, arms out, refusing to move, as another van turned up. Unlike me, he was fearless. The last I saw was Carl surrounded by police being marched off.

And the story he'd told me?

It was what I'd always known, but blanked. Not just *his* story, but all his friends too. It was how boys like him were treated at our school, and I'd deleted it. Every day they lined up outside the deputy head's office awaiting sanctions that he, in his flat-voiced wisdom called 'reasonable'. The boys were suspended, threatened with expulsion, then put on report and kept out of lessons. And they were all black. Every one of them. Black.

So how had I missed it?

Because I wanted to and because I'd persuaded myself that I was the victim and because that sort of thing didn't happen to people like me. There was a cheat in the system and I'd become part of it.

Yes, behind what I'm saying, I'd seen myself as fragile. White and fragile. But I know that's the lie and I'm lucky. Very lucky. And I've found myself out.

As for Carl? I never saw him again. But I think he'd recognised the cheat in the system and the lie I lived by. I hope he reads this story. In another way, I hope he doesn't.

Una Corda

4.

It was his secret. Because it was absurd and couldn't really happen it belonged to those voices he'd made up as a child, speaking of being chosen. There was always a chance, anything was possible; he'd believed that then. At four he'd his own private world, a place off-limits where everything was simple and the voices in his head told him he was *a name* – so why not at forty? Of course, as an adult he'd had to take a view, put himself out there as sensible and limited – D. Whittle, HR Manager, who people could depend on. Around the office he gave out advice, knew about procedure, told stories about panels who argued or didn't know how to score, and only touched on something real when he chatted during breaks about after-school clubs and children learning music. Then he was warm and bright and quietly made up. And in that mood, he could go the whole day with pieces he was practising running through his head – usually scales or early Mozart. But mostly it was meetings and meetings, with agendas and progress reports and emailed spreadsheets and the need to be in charge, so that his passion only showed when he closed his door. That was when he smiled. And his smile grew, becoming fixed and dreamy, as he slid the bolt and returned to his desk. This was his place, his own secret studio where he held out his hands, just above the surface, leaning forward. And when his hands began moving, he was the keyboard whizz, practising his pieces for his debut appearance.

But inside he was cold.

At home he waited until the children were in bed then began his practice with the soft pedal down. He called it his hour, but continued many more while his wife watched TV. There was strain now in his playing, a tremor, as he imagined her watching. She was in the audience, shaking her head and refusing to clap. More likely, of course, she wasn't much interested. So when he heard her on the stairs he carried on playing – quietly determined, expecting nothing. And when he finally joined her, Hazel was asleep and turned to the wall.

Next day she was curt.

"It's Friday, Daniel," she said while the children dressed.

He knew. This was her pass-out evening – a kind of payback, really, for what she put up with.

"Don't worry," he replied.

"I'm not," Hazel shot back, as if in surprise.

"Not?"

"I don't."

"You don't?"

"Won't."

"Won't what?"

"Worry."

Sometimes, he thought, they talked across each other like rival announcers.

"Seven o'clock," she added, and busied herself with the children.

During the day while Dan went to the office, Hazel worked from home. It suited her. There was no fixed timetable so she could input graphics and add to products while looking up TV times and messaging friends. She even sent an email to Dan checking how he was. And when he came home, she asked about his day then mentioned Denise and Sam, who'd both had issues at school – small stuff, of course, but something to watch for.

That evening, when she'd gone, Dan talked and played with the children and read a bedtime story before taking them upstairs. "Now clean your teeth and snuggle down," he called. "And sleep tight."

Afterwards, as he crept downstairs, he was in the clear. The children were asleep, Hazel was out, and in a moment he'd be playing. Sliding the door shut, he sat down at the keyboard. The room was quiet. Taking a breath, he adjusted his cuffs. This was his chance.

Suddenly, he was alone. He'd nothing to give, and as for the music – he'd never really played it. There was a gap between him and the piano. The keys – what were they? – black and white and silent. And if there'd ever been an audience, they'd all walked out. He was D. Whittle, HR Manager, who moved his hands and made up what he did.

It was his secret.

My generation

The escalator rises over bare blue space.
The hush takes us through.
Booked in, we're directed by name and floor
to wait behind blinds.

Butterfly exotics, spiked and twisted,
with big leaf wingspans
fill up the vases.

I'm here with partner to meet up with H_____,
Still standing, 40 years on.

My generation.

To look back and laugh
on wild times and drop-outs and turn-ons
and what it was to me,
or steps up and down,
liftshafts to the top, smooth-talk, viewpoints,
and how we are today.

The flowers, too, are well-bred.
Great glass drops hold off the mob.
Blue-chip, gilt-edged, high-risk, top-spot,
this is The City.

He arrives.
After handshakes, warm words
and two hours' catch-up
driven, high-pressure, by life-thoughts
and questions, he talks of dropping out

of wild-child dreams, growth and difference,
and sunlit heartlands living to be free.

We laugh. Leaving, we embrace.

He peace signs us out.
His eyes, grown large, follow us.
Red, red-orange and pressed against glass,
the flowerheads glow.

Mama, I Just Killed a Man

I'm told I could be heard inside my mother's belly. Kicking up, making a fuss, chuntering – well, that's what they said. I call it crying, but not the *I want* kind of screaming or the shock of cold air flooding into lungs. After all, if tears are warm water then that's what we are. And in my case, by the time I was born I'd cried myself out. So it all began with tears but like the weather it soon passed over.

At the start, they called me Boy. A Boy, You Boy, The Boy – plus several other sobriquets based on my proper name – George Robert William Harold Davis. Written out in full and entered as a password, it'd be considered strong. I was Georgie Porgy, Bob the Builder, William the Conqueror, Harold Wilson and Miles Davis – but then, what's in a name?

It was when I was sent off to boarding school that the real crying began. I acted the big man, keeping it quiet even to myself, but inside I was crying.

"Please be strong," my mother said when she visited. She knew I was struggling.

I nodded. Jen had brought me up to feel things her way. So I'd understood early on that she really wanted to help. Really is the word. There was a plea, a shaky, hyped-up insistence behind her smile, as if someone had let her down. Everything was So Important in Our House.

My strength was outward. It didn't really happen, of course. I learned how to fake it, to charge down the pitch, kick a ball and run off punching the skies. Later, I learned how to tighten my jaw and square my shoulders as if I was on film, or in a superhero comic. A dream, of course, because my whole self was pumped up so hard it hurt. When I became captain, I wore my armband as a sign that I knew the moves and had it all in hand. And I lived my own story. When I started at Law School, I dressed the part – blue shirt, black trousers and Italian shoes – and they called me Miles The Man. The nickname was courtesy of my fellow-student, Alex. Behind his smile he was a rebel, playing full-volume rockers like Jagger and Freddie Mercury – but they didn't touch me, not much. I was too squeamish. If I let go and lived it, I'd end up in a ball in a corner, hollering. So I got by, playing myself as a famous lawyer. When I stood up my voice was deep, and I spoke with power and weight, but inside I was crying.

What made me cry?

Being alone – which was pretty much all the time – and at arm's length from my mother and myself. Not that she didn't try, but she had too much troubling her and her heart was in her mouth. Her love was obsessive, compulsive and disordered. "Oh, look at yoohoo," she'd say, dressing me in a bow tie and blue stripy shirt. "Smile, my little man," she'd cry, and raise her arm, urging me to dance. That way, she said, I'd be the one who charmed her. When I'd danced and skipped to her satisfaction, she stood next to me, gazing in the mirror.

"You're my Jiminy Cricket," she said and started singing nursery rhymes. She told me she'd been on stage but her mother had put a block on it.

I remember once she took me to a children's party then stopped at the door.

"Promise, you won't cry," she said.

I glanced up at her, saying nothing.

"Even if they hurt you."

"Hurt me?"

Jen sighed, "They do that."

"They do?" I felt as if she'd found me out.

"Oh yes, they do horrid things."

Her warning was enough. The dangers I imagined made me fill up. From that day onwards I kept away from parties.

Like me, she was on her own. Whoever was my father, he was just a word. Daddy, him, or just Mr ____. It was as if he'd never existed. I grew up believing that I was hers and the messy business of making babies had never happened. I might have been living in a monastery.

What made me cry most were her stories.

She didn't exactly tell them to me. Not to my face. They were for her bedroom, told to her mirror with me listening at the door. They were full of loss and betrayal, spoken in a stage whisper, with gestures and tears.

And it was one of her stories that finished me. Told in the dark, it was about a fallen woman who was tried unjustly, labelled as a criminal and took her own life.

I was at home, playing my lawyer self. I was practising a summing up speech in the mirror while hearing
her story running in my head. The speech was calculated, but desperate really; a final appeal, for my client,
as well as me. We were up against a Hanging Judge. I
was defending a man who'd stolen an ID.

As I delivered my speech the tears began to flow. I'd
hidden everything and now I was exposed. I'd wanted
to please; to be someone else.

With that, I understood. I was in the dock myself.
A forgotten song went through my head *Mama, I just
killed a man*. I knew what had happened. I could see him
watching from the corner of my eye. My tears were for
_____ the judge.

5.

An eidetic poem.

Who is this man?

Inspired by a photo of a man with *Repeat Offender*
printed on his back looking out from an empty café
over Gloucester

My eye is drawn to the wedge of sky
outlining this man.
His shaved head shows up like a rock.

In his mind,
the blue and white seascape canvas
seen from the cell of his bedroom
takes him on a journey.

It's all part of the novel he's writing.

He's cloud-riding Odin
looking down at a darkened corner
where his childhood used to be.

His dream's inside, navigating the floating world
of high cirrus and whited church towers
to live forever on cool air.

Caught between light and dark, he hears
the door closing on jet-stream memories,
sees from the past,
the tops of trees stretching to the sky.

The voice of the poet comes out of words, and their quirks and oddities. It's rarely character-led, although the person speaking the lines is a powerful, ghostly presence.

The novel often presents a gallery of characters set in a particular time and place. The storyline examines who they are, where they're from and what they become, whereas the poem enters straight into soul.

Both are conventional but also collect unusual words, striking images and memorabilia. They follow their own rules, which are complex and exhaustive, but can be bent to effect – although with care; not over-or-understated.

There's a nowness about the novel; it's big and it's out there. The scenes are substantiated by detail and historical accuracy. The characters speak and act as representatives. It's a grand tour taking in history and psychology and generational difference and how we live now.

And the poem? Bursts of light, flowers, rituals, and memories in the dark.

"Fiction is dreaming up a different existence, poetry is shaping memory into significance." *Adam Thorpe*

Valentine's Poem

I

Daffodils are admirers,
they love each other's company
And seek out partners
whose shyness makes them strong.

See them in the sun!

A fieldful of watchers. Eyes, eyes
That dance without thought; Narcissus passionale.

For those of us who dream of being more:

Champagne on the dancefloor.

II

Wind, and they flare up;
Go all over; appear not to know things;
look the other way.

Then next-morning-lakeside,
sunstruck, firstime remembered,
Opening where they will.

Freshness we still touch

With Paper White, Bridal, February Gold.

"Our memory is a more perfect world than the universe: it gives back life to those who no longer exist." *Guy de Maupassant*

"No one has to explain a daffodil." *Picasso*

NARCISSI

Narcissi
showing flesh,
headstrong
in heels,
blow
hot
blow cold,
hairflick
and nod
in time to the wind,
springstep
and
surprised
with uplift
and admirers,
youthstruck
on a high
take aim
make eyes.

Finger lick
on
a

VIOLA

Thumb-sized,
patchy,
your
lost girl
look!
Memories,
perhaps,
of soul
in a crush,
eye-wide
or thoughtful,
of bruises
and confessionals
of stories
going round,
and the colours
of concealment
that soften
into sighs.
All earth
and darkness
in a
hand-bound

thread,
headturn
and glisten
bare light
and shiver
as shadows
scatter rain.

Big eyes
in
the
sun
look down
by water
up
in image,
dream
soul
in pictures
mirror their expressions
with come-hither glances
and words
of
approbation
without
a
thought
of
love.

book.

Is it
how you
are?
Toothy,
awkward,
on standby
by the fence,
an admirer
at a distance
whose desires
colour up,
blue-black,
purple, yellow,
dreaming of
indifference
opened
to a smile?
For those
Who seek
love

the darkness
of your
statements
will stand
the test
of time.

I'm sitting at my computer, looking down at the estate where I live. It's a square of green between yellow-brick flats. To the right, there's a parked-up access road and a footpath leading to a lawn with benches. It backs onto the fence of a large school. To the left, the flats form a three-storey perimeter wall. Beyond that a slope drops to a road into town. The estate is a 60s build with 43 households, an underground car park and wooden posts to protect the grass from vehicles.

As I look, I see several trees surrounded by grass. There's one tall Corsican Pine, a fir tree, an Amelanchier and a group of cherries. They're our friends. They watch over us and we watch over them. In the past some tenants wanted the trees chopped down. There were complaints about blocked views, lost light and dangerous roots. So when a sprawling copper beech shed a branch, they demanded action. It took months of debate followed by inspections and a report, then more debate and a scan of the tree before felling began.

I remember the tree surgeon climbing the trunk and firing up his chainsaw. He was a lithe, acrobatic giant and he scaled that tree like a roofer. I could see him as a stuntman or a net-and-trident gladiator. What followed was noisy and unrelenting. When the branches fell, they were stripped of leaves and dragged to a shredder where they were pulped. The air rang to the sound of metal against wood. When he reached the stump, it took several minutes to chop out each section. Afterwards, he left behind him a mud patch and a flattened plinth of wood. He had killed off the tree. It was an unpleasant way to go.

There are mushrooms now, sprouting around the stump. They come up in small, fist-like clumps, and stay for a while. They are visitors from below, feeding on leftovers. They repurpose life.

At this time of day with the sun still low, the view seems fixed. It's a reserved space. A green island where people and animals and plants come together. It's the home to bluetits, grey squirrels, jackdaws and overfed cats. I've seen the space invaded by crows, swooping in low to hot-tail squirrels. But the squirrels were clever. Their constant swerves kept them safe. The crows dived in, the squirrels set off, and the two ran Keystone Cop races.

I saw a woodpecker early one morning hunting for worms. It was shuffling forward and nodding its head like a clockwork model. Another day I saw a blue and orange jay balanced on the fence by the school. It flew onto a branch then into bushes. Both were closed-off and otherworldly. More recently, I witnessed a scrum between crows and kites, foraging for meat put out by a neighbour. The kites winged in, circling and dropping suddenly from tree-height, but within seconds the crows came mobhanded to chase them off. It felt like an episode from a wildlife film.

Contra Naturam

15/05/21 Gaza Bombing

I'm looking.

Seen through glass
between parked cars and brickwork,
red kites and crows mob on the grass.

Diving for meat on a clipped lawn
they're scrapping.

The crows have numbers on their side.
They push and swagger and brawl like flies.

The kites are dancers who glide full circle
then dive side-on in a death drop.

And I'm at my computer, watching.

The birds live in snatches. Balls in the air,
they pick and spin and fly free.
They're blackshirts and reds in a standoff.

While on screen there are flashes.
Fire eats bodies. Lynch mobs roam the streets.
Planes and rockets shower down hits.

I'm looking.

As the day goes on the people come out of their front doors. Young and old, I know them well, some by sight, some by name. It's tidal, beginning with the early-morning runners wearing wristbands and headphones, followed by commuters carrying umbrellas and bags, and drivers with keys and phones. Later, the parents walk their children to school, then shoppers appear – usually elderly – while delivery vans turn up and workmen arrive. When the bins show up, they reverse in and block the road while loading. The men who do it work fast, seizing heavy bags and piling them into the back of the lorry. Some bags had been holed by crows, scattering their contents.

In the early afternoon there's usually a lull but after that the tide flow reverses with residents returning, a late postie appearing, and children playing until early evening; then it's lights on, a few latecomers, and darkness.

Next morning the grass has been dug into craters. It looks like someone has taken a golf club to the lawn. If so, it seems our golfer wanted something. A treasure hunt perhaps? Or a soil test? But the holes' outlines suggest something else. This is not about golfers or gardeners or people chasing gold. They're paw marks.

I'm still sitting at the window, but now it's night time and a grey shape is circling the lawn. I don't see any digging, but it's head down, sniffing. It feels very old. In the dark it could be something remembered, an idea coming out of my head. Whatever it *really* is, I know it's an animal I've seen before, because it comes round here often. And although it's a fox, it's also a mystery and a symbol. It's part of what I share with life.

"The impulse to find the likeness between unlike things is very basic to us, and it is out of that, of course, which the simile or metaphor springs. So a poem moves towards
some sort of clarification, and the creation of a space in which sense,
however fleetingly, may be made." *Paul Muldoon*

Affirmations for Earth

I   *The Fly*

What am I like? Compact, telescopic,
I write at all angles, zigzag and shake
to a side-stepping, fly-buzzing shuffle
where I'm in the zone.

Sometimes, hiding, I go dark, ease myself down
into cracks, while keeping things covered
from the corner of my eye.
I'm the fly who never was.

Then I'm in the fast lane
in a wildside runaway dream
of slips and happenstance
and by-chance growths
where small is large and strange is the norm.

Living is my passion. I'm cutting through air
as the hot-foot bow-boy messenger who appears
from nowhere, arriving in a helmet and a mask.

But mostly I'm the kid, the slab-faced watcher
who sees what's there, measuring the growth
of age-lines and hairs,
and the turned-down corners

of time and truth covered by a smile
– they're in there if you look.

So, what's blue-black-and-grey
with a forest of arms, dances on points
and leaps like a deer when things kick off

and can easily outsmart you?

II   *In the woods*

Listen, say the trees, what's that sound?
A slow drip trickle of breath
that drifts and spreads, wafting over ramsons.

Something in the flow and dull calm weight
filling up the air with white-starred bits.
A closed-up world quietly pressing in,
putting up doors and arches.

Look up, they say, it's a map
of clouds and hanging gardens.

Look around, it's a tai chi class
greeting the sunrise with both arms raised.

Look down and it's a chain: a sweet, square root
feeding on water and carbon
that it pillars into rock.

The trees are our old folk.
They hang out their banners
saying *Green*. They come bearing gifts.

III   *Earthworms*

Are original. They rise from the bottom.
Heavy-jawed and forcing they open up earth.

Once dug in, they work by feel, absorbing
themselves in the invisible spectrum.
Part of the kingdom, they minister to the dark.

Whale-mouth feeding they swell up.
Blindly, like the tree, like the fly,
and belly-down-grazing
they filter dirt.

On them rests the world.

1.

Living in flats, we get to know things the world
doesn't see. In our block the walls are thin, so when
voices are raised it becomes an open-house event.
Sometimes it's hard to tell whether the shouts come
from a turned-up TV or the neighbours arguing. A
row on one side went on once for an hour with both
sides cutting in and hardly a pause for breath. Things
were said that most soaps would edit out. What was
surprising was how the couple seemed to operate in

their own private space. The mike was on, but they didn't seem to know it.

The tenant before them would launch into angry, sweary tirades, shouting abuse at on-screen football. Outwardly he was reasonable, sociable and community-minded; inwardly he was ready to explode. In his case, football brought out his alter ego, but also being at home switched off his social awareness. To him, it was all the same whether he was shouting at a screen or on the terraces.

In both these examples the action happened like a studio outtake, with the actors off-script, and us as unseen sound crew. Although, in the case of the rowing couple, their arguments soon gave way to slamming doors and high-volume TV. It was if they'd cancelled everything and switched channels.

But then everything changed. It was when I saw our neighbour on the other side being helped indoors by two care workers. She had her back to me, but I could tell she was upset. In the past I'd seen her as a frail old lady walking slowly, but this time, as she entered her flat, she was yelling.

I'd come across that noise before with an elderly woman I used to walk. She would call out to an imaginary audience, making whistling noises and heehawing. It wasn't quite a carnival or a solo performance, more like holding up a notice saying she was alive.

That evening the noise began. It sounded like a noir film, played full volume. "HELLO," falsetto, quivering. "HELLO," again, louder. "HELLO," shouted and repeated every few seconds. "HELLO," at a shriek.

At first we put up with it. When something unexpected happens, it can take time before it sinks in. But by the next day, we were beginning to realise that the shouts weren't going away. There were quiet patches and loud passages and mysterious thumps and scrabbling noises and a feeling all the while of being close to something awful. It was like living through a murder mystery.

When I spoke to the care workers, I learned that their visits were timed and she was calling them back. At their suggestion, I kept a tally of her shouts and emailed them to the manager. To begin with she clocked up 60 – 70 shouts per episode, but over time the frequency dropped. What had seemed a huge threat turned into a personal reaction – a minor kind of 'tester', for me as well as her. In the end I could hear her talking quietly to her carers.

Our elderly neighbour was another example of what happens when the mind takes over and what's said belongs to a category of one.

We all have our moments where we think – and sometimes say – things we regret. They're the badmouth voices that find a way in, usually at times of stress. Quite often they're LOL and cartoon-ish. But as they become habitual, we stop hearing ourselves. One spat runs into another and they're quickly forgotten. Or rewritten. Or simply denied. So, when my first couple stopped shouting, their default was silence, as if nothing had happened. In the case of our elderly neighbour she had to learn, like me, that we're stronger than we think.

The point is to stay conscious.

2.

Bev and Naomi were sitting in a corner of their local coffee shop. To their right, a couple were chatting over a wooden table; directly opposite, a pregnant woman was standing in the doorway; to their left, two men on stools were reading newspapers; while beyond them, and close to the door, a woman in joggers was talking on her phone.

For Bev and Naomi this was their spot, where they held the space, made their statements, and set the world to rights.

"Busy in town," said Bev, checking her topknot.

Outside, it was a mild February morning, and a couple with a dog and a pair of walkers were sitting around tables. The road beyond was queued up with idling vehicles.

"And inside," Naomi answered, looking down the room.

The café was arranged like a living room/diner. Where they sat it was wider with a double row of tables leading to a counter; further in, the tables were smaller with cushioned wall seats and wickerwork chairs; there were flowers in vases, decorated tablemats and art on the walls.

Bev took a pen from her handbag. "What do you think they're thinking?" she asked, opening a notebook.

Naomi glanced around. "What's who thinking?"

"These in here. If they're willing to."

"To think?"

"Or not. That is the question."

"No, Bev, please. You can't say that."

"I can't?"

"Well, you shouldn't."

"But I can think it?"

"Haha, maybe. But keep it close. Between ourselves."

Bev frowned. "I'll try," she said, bending forward. Her hand shook as she put pen to paper.

Naomi returned to sipping her coffee. Her friend's face, while she wrote, had the concentrated look of a child working at a difficult task. Every so often, she crossed out something or added a phrase in capitals.

Suddenly, Bev put down her pen. "It's what they're not thinking that bothers me," she said, flatly.

"You on that again?"

"Pretending. Head in the sand. I'm all right Jack. Blanking, big time."

"But is it so – or an act?"

"Whatever. See no evil, hear no evil, and it all goes away."

When Angela entered the café a voice in her head said standing room only. But as she lined up to order, she realised that was wrong. This wasn't like happy hour or a packed train. In fact, although the room was buzzing, it was quiet as well. Typical, she thought, of a politeness-first provincial town with nothing much to shout about. Just like the song, *Heaven is a place where nothing ever happens.*

In any case everyone's number was up.

"Would you like to order?" asked the red-haired woman behind the counter. She was smiling.

Angela frowned. What on earth did she mean? Order what? Certainly, there were things she'd like to have but they weren't on the menu. "Oh, anything – flat white with oat milk will do."

"Drink in or take away?"

"In."

"We'll bring it to you." The smile had faded slightly to half-moon, third quarter. "Would you like anything else?"

Angela shook her head.

When the woman confirmed, Angela pulled out her card. As it bleeped against the glass, something passed through her. There were things she couldn't say.

As she checked the tables, a group stood up. It happened in unison, as if they'd rehearsed it. Sitting down, Angela imitated the barista's smile. This was her disguise. She was the short, freckle-faced woman who wasn't there. Ms Average. A stand-in in a film, or a face at a window. Of course, living here, she saw what went on – the march to the station, daytime school runs, shopping, phoning, commuting in the dark – it was all so reassuring and neatly tied up. A trap to catch flies.

A waiter came up. "Flat white with oat milk?"

Nodding, Angela pointed to the table. Better to say nothing.

But as she sipped her coffee, the thoughts took over. *Entitlement. Cynicism. Everything sucks.* The song she heard was *Money, money, money.* Because people in Deepling Gate did too much, spent too much and wanted the Moon. In fact, she wondered why she'd come here at all. What was she doing in a MOR town of well-off people chasing their tails?

Suddenly, hearing a voice, she got to her feet. It was harshly insistent, telling her to listen. Right up close but far away as well. And distorted. But of course, she knew who was speaking. Her father, pulling her up. Only this was *her* turn. "No!" she called, as she stepped on a chair and onto the table. It felt like she was preparing to jump.

"Coffee?" she shouted. "Coffee-coffee-coffee!" She was sounding the alarm. "What's it about a stupid cup that you spend so much time on it? And money of course. Money-money-money!"

The room hushed as if a gunman had entered. All eyes were on her.

"What's the use of anything at all? Coffee, coffee, coffee. Money, money, money – whoohoo! That's all you ever think of."

By now two staff had reached the table. They were red-faced and short of breath.

"Listen everyone. There's a climate emergency. and you're all zonked out. Yes, it's the business now.

Code red. A death spiral. And what are you lot doing? Sitting drinking and talking like nothing's happening."

One of the staff members waved her down. But she knew they couldn't touch her. This was a crime scene, and she was the cat in a tree.

"Oh hoho! Chop, chop. Are you hearing me now? The planet's burning – dying – we're just about dead, kaput, and you lot are in your cups."

Angela squeezed her hands together. They were her batteries, charging. Like vessels, they contained her grief. When the moment came, they'd lose all feeling.

Her voice dropped low. "But I can tell. You're not even with me. Not in your hearts. Not so you feel it. It's all out there, a sham, just nice coffee lip service and on to the next dream."

She shivered as a hand tugged at her jeans. "And don't touch me, you lot, don't damned touch me!" Swearing, she kicked over her cup.

The coffee spread in dark pools. It was nut-brown and smeary like molasses.

"See, oil!" she shouted, squatting down and coating her hands. "Oily-oil. That's what's doing it." She laughed, finger-smearing her face. The streaks were her warpaint.

"I'm done," she said, backstepping onto the chair. "You lot are done," she added, descending to the floor. Her movements had slowed and her voice had dropped to a whisper. "And don't say I didn't tell you."

In the corner of the coffee shop, Bev and Naomi were on their feet. Bev was waving her notebook and Naomi was holding up her cup in toast position. Both were breathing hard. To their right, a couple were shouting questions at each other; directly opposite, a pregnant woman was doubled over, holding her stomach; to their left, two men on stools were raising their fists; while beyond them, and close to the door, a woman in joggers was crying.

Moving Images

The soundtrack to the film
2050 The Last Generation Speaks has been lost.

It vanished with the artworks
of the London and New York galleries
and the burnt-out desert-stops
of Angkor Watt and Great Zimbabwe.

Like a cry in a storm it came and went
then spread upwards on light wings,
to hover as a message in the sky
warning of Easter Island and Mohenjo-Daro.

It had served its purpose.

For us, it was a film in the head, rerun so often
that the images had become hand-of-God slides
streamed at all hours onto walls and ceilings.

Seen by the elderly it flashed up 1930s photos
of empty shelves and queues at the bank.

Reviewed by the screen buffs
it was a switch from unreal horror
to a death in the living room,
while for the dedicated gamers it was WW3

fought for real in hand-to-mouth emergencies.

But then came the remake. Pieced together
from memory and scraps left over,
it told the history of die-ins, vigils,
lock-ons and ceremonial occupations,
and the worldwide Children's March
from capital to capital
that brought things to a stop.

And now, in playback, we're caught on camera
blocking traffic, flesh against metal,
protecting the wild, then talking Satyagraha
and being the change you want to see,
as we walk with Siddhartha in the woods
while hearing the sound of
trees in the wind, rain on grass, animals feeding.

3.

Often, as I fall asleep, I find myself 'thinking in film'.
The pictures I see are clips from documentaries and
late-night dramas, crossed with cartoons. Sometimes
I merge everyday scenes with imaginary locations and
faces from the past – all re-sized and lopsided, as in a hall
of mirrors. It's an air-collage drawn from gardens and
beaches, seen through the eyes of a child, with jumps
into dark holes to crawl through tunnels and bunkers.
And around the edges, or just outside the picture, are
the watchers. They're the walk-on acts that didn't quite
make it. The ghosts of what might have been. I call

them my director's cut. As Scorsese says, "It's a matter of what's in the frame and what's out."

Thinking in images is the norm today. In our heads, we're on screen 24/7, so what we see is what we are. We view our photos, see through the lens, watch replays, and sample the world in snapshots, icons, memes, selfies and screenshots. Our buzzwords are *point of view, I'll put you in the picture* and *show don't tell*. The aim is mimetic. To record with camera-like clarity, telling it as it is. But of course, the mirror isn't real, the image is CGI, and the seeming-solid appearance is a trick of the light. And everything we see is given meaning by what we know.

To quote Macbeth (as he's hallucinating) either our eyes "…are made the fools o' the other senses,/ or else worth all the rest."

....

It's early morning and I'm standing in the kitchen holding a small plastic bottle. The label on it says *Ganfort*. It's an eye medicine. One I know is powerful. The prescribing doctor warned it might hurt. So I'm extra careful as I pull down my eyelid and squeeze in a drop. But when the drop lands, it tickles, as if someone had doused my eye with warm water. I blink, then following instructions, close my eye and finger-press the corner. I can feel where bone meets flesh.

I keep my finger there for two minutes, counting. The instructions say it's to stop the medicine reaching the rest of my body. I wonder what's in it and think of toxic chemicals. I remember drops that burned or caked-up my eyelashes, and others that made me tired all the time.

I switch the bottle to my left eye. As the drop lands, I'm seeing the field test printout. It was covered in crosses. I'd scored a duck.

After treating both eyes, I sit down. My view has changed. The room looks slightly odd and the angles have softened. It's as if I'm peering through a dirty window. Of course, I know what's happening: my sight's draining away.

When I first learned that I had glaucoma I was prescribed *Tafluprost*. Despite being weaker than *Ganfort*, the drops worked – but with side effects, caused by preservative. When I took them at night, I'd wake with my eyelids stuck together. It resembled what my parents called 'sleepy dust'. But this was closer to being in a plaster cast. Removing it was like scraping wallpaper, and brought hairs with it. What kept me going was my belief that the treatment was temporary.

Later, when I spoke to my doctor, the truth came out. As he switched me to preservative-free drops he said, "They're for life." At first, I didn't believe him. Surely there must have been a mistake? But as I left the clinic, the words sank in. Perhaps I'd known it all along? Or maybe I'd been told, but missed it. Even then, at a deeper level, I was angry. Why had this happened to me? I asked myself. It felt like an unjust punishment.

Over the next few years, I used the drops every morning, squeezing them into my eyes. *Tafluprost* didn't hurt and felt a bit like an old-fashioned eyebath. When my annual check-up came round, I stared into a simulator, pressing a clicker when I saw a flash. Afterwards the doctor directed a white light into my eyes, then floated a disc onto my cornea. The field test was bearable, the light didn't hurt, but the disc – despite the anaesthetic – required clenched teeth.

On all the visits, my pressures were good and my eyesight stable. So when the appointments stopped, I continued the treatment, telling myself I was fine, and when my vision blurred I blamed it on ageing. Even when my left eye misted up, I put it down to cataracts. It was only when I couldn't read medium-size print that I went to the optician. She referred me. The result is what I live with today.

Looking back, my dad suffered from glaucoma, but for a long time it remained undetected. He was a tall, serious, dark-haired man who sat next to the window in his high-backed chair, reading. Nothing suggested that he was struggling to see. He'd been a good sportsman and a surveyor during WWII and his thick black glasses gave him gravitas. He was a sensible, rational man who'd survived the Western Desert, but for him Glaucoma was a stealth attack that went undetected. He wasn't given tests, and when he complained, the optician simply changed his glasses. It was only after his death that I realised that he'd been sitting there for at least a year without a book.

Glaucoma is a one-way trip. If you don't spot it early, all you can do is limit the damage. In my case, I feel let down. *Ganfort* works better than *Tafluprost*, but it can't bring back what I've lost. There's a freeze-frame, lights-down feel about it, as if I'm alone, walking into nowhere. It reminds me of playing in the garden, stalking my own shadow. When the clouds come over, I hide behind bushes. With nothing to go on, I'm invisible. There's danger all around. I've lost my way, and need to keep direction and talk myself up. The world I've taken for granted is no longer there. It's like opening a black box with my name on it.

A book follows its own logic; the writer's task is to see it through. The rule is: say it once then move on. Too much signposting what's happening and keeping the reader onside doesn't work.

Writing is a slow, hermetic exploration of your own limits. And the opportunity to revise a book is a building process where each added layer cements the last, bonding it together and strengthening the whole.

What emerges is bigger than the personality of the author.

And then there's the protest gear.

Placards made of carboard stacked on top of wardrobes with plywood poles sticking out. Orange flags with hourglass designs, propped up in corners and tied with string like kites. Battered cardboard boxes full of leaflets behind doors with bags beside them – some of them scrawled on – containing posters and banners and stickers in reels. And a litter of bust cards, badges, petitions and speech notes on paper.

It's a bit of a backstage costume store.

And the colours? Primary mainly, with blue-black lettering and graphics in red.

Sometimes I picture our protest gear in a museum, dated and labelled behind glass for curious grandchildren (if there are any). I imagine them as artefacts, dug up from a lost way of life. There are sticks, cardboard squares, scraps of cloth and paper, some patched, some water-stained, mostly torn. What holds them together is their message.

Looking at them now, crammed into corners, they seem like fragments from a tale waiting to be told.

And the ending to their story?

They might be what's left over. Relics, pointing to what happened. Or they might be the charms that saved us. Whatever they are, they're power in our hands. We carry them into action as our talismans. Like pennies in a pot, they add up.

Extinction Rebellion, London Occupation 2019

I remember
where we nested on trucks
with our talons drilled into metal
as we sent up wild cries calling to our children,
and they gathered,
rising from their bedrooms
and playgrounds and schoolrooms
to fold their wings around the wounds
and consecrated body of Earth our host.

How we made tarmac into garden,
seeding ourselves in the night
and easing up next morning
through drains and cracks
to release soft balsamic fragrance
and love-repeat blooms
unlocking who we are.

Yes, I remember how we offered ourselves,
sitting cross-legged on stony ground
held together by our songbooks and testimonies
and the rising tide of quiet
on the bridge and in the Square,
and in the silent wait at the Circus
for leaf-boat rescue.

And in that minute, as I watched,
the air became an Arch,
the sun told the truth; the traffic stopped
and the trees and protestors stood tall
raising a dream-song space with their bodies,
while all the birds
of Oxfordshire and Gloucestershire
sang emergency.

"Poetry purifies the language of the
tribe." *Stéphane Mallarmé*

Glaucoma

For Paralympian cyclist James Brown with limited vision who climbed on a plane at City Airport, London, in climate protest

I

I'm in the kitchen
pressing a dropper to my eye.

It's a magical corrective.

There are metaphors here
of darkness visible and groping for the alarm.

At the back of everything
is our dream of having more.
Or less. Or nothing.
And how soon will it be?

II

At 5% this man's vision was perfect.

He climbed on a plane in full view.

Up there he saw it all – the big swings
and blows into death drops, falling,

with contact lost and things breaking up.

Speedups. Overruns. Blowouts.
Look and you will see.

But for now, he's holding off the crash
with an eye to what's to come,
riding for team climate.

III

Everyone has their time.

His came with a grip, a foothold and an up.

Once there, he was the bare-back rider
with his body at full stretch
owning the race for his children

and for the narrow band we live in.

For the busy VIP passengers,
he was code red.

IV

When the nurse calls my name
I'm for the field test.

With one eye shut, I fit my chin to a bar.
In my hand's a clicker. Now, count.

The stars I'm seeing are messages
from planets that once held life.
Their inhabitants took what they could.
They'd used up everything by the time they hit
the wall.

Each new burst is an *ah*.

A Glass, Darkly

Maybe I'll go to heaven for this. After all, what we did was driven by love, and in any case, it was our wedding anniversary. I do remember how everything speeded up as we approached the action. Life had become immediate, changeable, fast-tracked, full-on. But when the glass went, it seemed like the end.

To understand what happened, you need to know that Sue and I are climate rebels and we park our small hatchback in a garage with an up-and-over metal swing door.

It all began on September 1st 2020, XR occupation day. I'd not slept well and felt a flutter of anxiety boarding the train, until I saw that the carriage was largely empty. But when we changed to the underground, despite the masks, the closeness was alarming. It was as if all the passengers were attached invisibly to one giant ventilator or we were in a wind tunnel being tested. Everything was dark and out of our control. Although, in truth, lots of young people in London seem to think they're immortal. As an elderly person I probably should have stayed at home.

But our young rebels weren't like that. They were shy, gentle, feeling types who had come out on the streets to sound the alarm. So, when we paraded from Trafalgar to Parliament Square, the walls and buildings shook to the drums and whistles of the Samba band and the pumped-up shouts of 'Climate Justice Now'.

Our pace quickened as we approached Parliament Square. Looking back, I could see flags and banners and marching crowds, while ahead there were lines of police. When they stopped us, I thought of pushing through, but then they allowed us in, waving towards the central green. It was at that moment, without saying anything, that everyone sat down in the road.

To be honest, it didn't happen quite like that. There's a tension between what goes into a story and the truth. In life things are random and messy, in the story everything ties up. So even though I didn't see the rebels take the road, in my mind it happened as a single spontaneous action. In XR we talk and theorise but then an idea pops up and everyone acts together. It's like those moments when Sue and I have the same thought simultaneously. It's a sharing of love.

While Sue occupied the road, I went to find my friend Julian, catching up with him by the Nelson Mandela statue. Julian's a blues musician and an environmental architect. He has a kind, bearded, teddy-bear-friendly face and a strong, ageing, slightly-out-of-shape body. Meeting him was a lift.

Julian pointed to his backpack. It had poles sticking out and a bagged-up mixer slung underneath.

"The rucksack PA," he said, easing it down onto a wall.

"I'm impressed," I said, tugging at a strap. "It looks heavy."

"Lighter than I thought."

"You've carried it a long way?"

"From Trafalgar. Didn't think I'd manage it, but you know, where there's a will..."

"It's the rebel in you."

Soon afterwards, the main PA arrived. Housed in a rickshaw, it drew up on the terrace, pumping out music to the crowd on the grass. As the speeches began, Julian and I circled behind the stage, broadcasting for the people in the road. We were the street corner crew, busking our messages of love and protest. I remember saying to our singer-songwriters, you can appear anywhere if you can get up on an XR stage. The crowd, of course, were totally with us.

When Sue was arrested, I was on the mike. She'd been surrounded and warned by an officer then, out of the corner of my eye, I saw the police lift her. As they carried her past me, I spoke about non-violence and necessary sacrifice. My busyness kept me from following her.

For the rest of the day, Julian and I worked as promoters and roadies. While I played advocate, boosting the performers, setting them up and enthusing the audience, Julian connected leads and adjusted the volume. As host and techie, we kept on the move, evading the police to preserve our equipment. We even took ourselves off to an XR Grandparents' action, crossing St James's Park to set up beside the huge, all-white Buckingham Palace fountain.

It was later, when I heard that Sue had been taken to Wandsworth Police Station, that I told Julian.

"You must go," he said. "Duty – no, love – calls."

I understood what he meant. Julian has a gentle, unquestioning, admiring way with his wife that mixes long looks with jokey affection – something Sue and I share, though we're more on-the-surface and febrile – and at that moment I'd begun to fear for her, even though we'd both been arrested before and knew what to expect.

"Thank you," I said, miming a hug.

Julian smiled. "Go."

As I left, I remembered how we'd met at the October occupation, moving a small PA on a pallet from road to park and then into hiding as the police lines advanced. They'd driven us before them, taking left-over tents and sleeping bags and anything else they could lay their hands on. Their intention had been clearance, but we kept one step ahead.

Leaving Parliament Square wasn't so easy. All but one exit was blocked by squads of officers. It was as if they'd become the protestors and were massing for action. For them, we were children who needed restraint.

I remember one skinny, rough-faced rebel yelling at them as he moved along their lines like an inspecting officer. He seemed to be shouting at someone inside his own head. One policeman turned his back, the others ignored him.

It took three attempts to get out of the square. The police had turned surly, blocking my way and threatening to arrest me. After a long detour to find a tube, I began my journey home with aching legs. I'd a pain in my back and I was shaky. When the train stopped mid-tunnel, I sat, staring into blackness. There was a long way to go; the people in the carriage weren't really there; in the dark I was alone.

....

In Gillain's dream she'd always been a rebel. It was how she was from the start – herself, nicely divergent, and different. There'd been no pink unicorns, floral dresses or magic wands, and she didn't do bows or ribbons or hair extensions. Now, at twelve, when it came to dressing up she wore cut-down shorts and ties without a collar. A year ago she'd switched from running shoes to home-made sandals, then shaved her head. She looked like a younger version of Grace Jones.

With her sister Fleur they were super-activists. It was their thing.

They walked to school, gave away their presents and checked things bought for animal products. Being bookish, they read about weather, measuring wind speed and temperature in the garden, and drew pictures of their findings. They called themselves *Wild Protectors* and danced and sang with their brother Dev at youth demonstrations where they struck up rhythms on pots and pans.

The dream began as they were working on a picture made of old tennis balls and cut-up boxes.

During a break, Gillain held up a book.

"What's that?" asked Fleur, pointing. The cover was red and black with green dots. At the bottom, in orange, were the words THE BOOK OF CLIMATE.

"It's about Earth, burning."

"No. Tha's horrible. What's it like inside?"

Without warning, they stepped inside the book.

"Is this real?" asked Fleur. The pages were full of strange-shaped graphs and pie charts. They were 3D and elastic, moving like snakes. In the background, the lines and colours sprouted like pot plants. It felt like a computer game.

"See. The captions," said Gillain.

Underneath the diagrams were words like 'species decline' and 'climate breakdown' in capitals.

"Is this happening?" asked Fleur.

The background had changed. A grey mist had set in. It felt like they were staring at an old wall.

"Whitewash," said Gillain. "And we're for it."

"It's a message," said Fleur.

"See," replied Gillain, pointing. They were inside a film, looking down on cracked roads and closed-up buildings. It was as if they were flying across where they lived – but seeing only empty streets and torched vehicles. "It's all in the book," Gillain said, and began to cry.

Fleur kept turning the pages. She was shaking her head. "What we always said."

Dust was settling in the park below. The lawns were baked brown and leaves hung from trees like used tissues.

"And it's a mega-crime," Fleur added.

"What we do now?" asked Gillain.

"We tell the truth."

"Like we just seen?"

"With everything we've got."

"But is there a point? Isn't too late?"

"Hey-hey, Gil. Shape up."

"But I'm afraid."

"You are? I never thought. Well, fact is I'm scared too."

In the silence that followed the two girls hugged.

"No, listen. The dream's right," Gillain said, closing the book. "It's time to shout."

"What – about this?" asked Fleur, pointing to their picture.

On the floor was a map of Earth mounted on card. It had mock-shells made of earrings, waves made of scarfs and spot-coloured continents using discarded makeup.

"Needs words," said Gillain, pulling out marker pens from a drawer. "Big ones. In colour."

"Fires too," said Fleur, selecting crayons from a box.

While Gillain wrote underneath CLIMATE EMERGENCY, Fleur filled up the corners with orange flames.

"It's good," said Gillain, stepping back.

"Good enough?"

"If we sing and dance and push it in their faces."

"Before it's too late."

"Now?"

"Yes. Now."

Holding up their picture, Gillain and Fleur walked out into their street, dressed in black. They were shouting.

....

When I think back to my childhood in Goma, Spring and Autumn brought the rains. With us now, drought eats the land. I remember the fields of green and yellow when I was Charles the lucky-boy. Now, the soil is hard and barren and there are storms bringing down landslides into the lake. So much has changed. But working as an agricultural collective, we survive,

Let me give you an example. As a group, we go out to plant trees – 17,000 last year – and we learn in schools and in churches about the environment. We get together as a people for the planet. If there's a shadow behind us, we face forward, even in the middle of war and climate breakdown. And we help those in need, for instance the people of Nyiragongo where they have to walk 25 km to get water. When we publicised their struggle, everyone gave them a helping hand.

We all do our bit. The clock of our lives is set to now. The work we do is difficult, but our bodies are strong. We uplift each other, as friends, not as competitors. Our way is more personal and less driven by profit than large-scale mechanized agriculture or factory farming.

When food was short, we started up kitchen gardens in the households and schools of Goma. Day on day we dug for plants and water. And we reached out to the starving people in the territories of Masisi and Kalehe, telling the world and getting action to save them.

Everyone counts, no one is missed out. A third of our political positions are reserved for women. Maybe in practice we don't achieve the full quota, but there are women who apply as deputies and pass, and the question of equality is treated seriously.

I wasn't born a farmer, but working with them has opened my eyes. They show us how to do things differently – and we learn from their lived experiences. One thing is sure, we don't teach rural communities, but we can help them to develop. It is they who have the knowledge.

Nature also has its realities: the more we advance, the more it changes – and as we go forward, the bare earth is transformed into a living land. We cannot return to the old world of my childhood, but we can put down roots and help each other. As a people we are blessed.

We do what we do out of love.

....

Paradise Lost

As a result of rising sea levels, East Island
in the French Frigate Shoals was washed
away by hurricane Walaka, Oct 2018.

I

The hot tub fills up.

Out in the Pacific,
an island floats on its shadow.

The line has narrowed.
Staring into brightness, we soak up warmth.

We've stayed in too long.

Half a mile of sand, safe till now,
rest stop and refuge for seals and turtles,
has melted into nothing.

II

The storm took it, leaving us behind.

Mixed roots, stems, eggshells,
the prints of crabs and urchins,
coral, anemone and worms,

the full envelope of life,
now torn apart and scattered,
dissolves into air

leaving behind a space
where in dreams we mouth the words
from ball games in yards

Can we have it back, please?

III

Invisible now,
we've only the maps as proof.

Lying low in huge blue,
you were all salt and undertow.

Your story: the stars, deep sea drift
and Oceania ancestors
going down with the sun.

Memories of the Gods.

. . . .

The letterboxes were all different. Some were silver lids
that just flapped up, often noisily; others were black
and stiffly resistant, opening inwards; some acted like
mousetraps, pinching flesh or scraping knuckles; many

had additional bristles or backplates that blocked, and some just didn't work.

But did it matter? After all, delivering leaflets about climate was voluntary, and once inside they'd probably go missing or be binned, unread. In fact, at times, Suzi suspected there were people waiting just behind the door, ready to pounce. Sometimes, as she walked away, she heard a clatter as a hand yanked a leaflet out of the box. That usually brought up a picture of an elderly male but in some neighbourhoods the person she saw was well-to-do and young. It was hard not to feel watched behind those closed doors. But when she came across windows full of children's artworks or rainbow stickers, Suzi smiled. People were good and well-intentioned, the sun was out – and even when the clouds rolled over their hearts stayed warm.

Of course, Suzi knew that she projected. As a child she'd loved her dad and shared his passions. He was an actor and told her about the need to be real and present and creative even when it didn't matter. He often quoted Meisner and talked a lot about empathy and finding out for yourself. So, when she went door to door, she told herself to simply be, to understand people and listen to their stories.

Turning a corner, Suzi crossed the road. Here the houses had short front gardens with steps up and low front doors. As she approached, she prepared herself for her *letterbox moves*. With some, at floor level, the trick was to squat, the little ones were fiddly, while the sideways slots took time. Then there were the outside boxes – some jammed, some locked like safes – and the doors without any kind of opening at all.

Also there were the dogs. Hounds out of hell, she called them – although only some, the big ones, who crashed against the door. Smaller dogs were tricksters. They yapped or yelped as if they'd been trodden on or scrabbled madly at the window. But the worst were the sneak-dogs who lay in wait then clamped onto leaflets.

Though at least they were awake, she thought, which was more than their owners. Until, of course, the barking began.

Reaching an estate, Suzi took the stairs to the top. That way, if someone came out, she could run. Well, perhaps not run, she told herself, but exit quickly without too much fuss.

Climbing to the top, she checked the layout – a balcony with one central staircase and doors both sides. In her mind she was undercover. As she posted through the doors, she could hear people inside. They didn't sound happy.

After the flats, Suzi began to miss out doors. They were the ones with curtains drawn and overgrown hedges, or stickers on the letterbox saying NO JUNK MAIL. Some of them red-lettered any kind of contact, threatening police action. They made her think of the warning notices she'd seen on woodland walks: KEEP OUT, PRIVATE and TRESPASSERS WILL BE PROSECUTED.

Reaching the end of the road and finding herself with some leaflets in hand, Suzi paused. She could hear her dad, talking about acting. His voice was telling her to *be*. It was all about living – just that, no more – and, of course, imagination.

Retracing her steps to the doors she'd missed out, Suzi folded the first leaflet in half and started posting.

....

On TV, there's a late-night show about climate change. It opens with soothing music and shots of a brightly-lit room. As the camera closes on the stage, the panellists are introduced by the host. They nod and smile in turn, projecting calm. But behind their masks there's another story. Look into their eyes and you'll see forests burning and cities underwater. Beyond that: landslides, uprooted trees, flattened crops. It's too deep and awful for words.

After a low-key start, our panellists become edgy, like families who can't get on. Leaning forward, they blank each other and address the camera. There's a formality about their words, as if they're actors running through a script. Behind their speeches is silence.

In the controllers' room they're talking about tone and balance. As the producer switches cameras, he's searching for soundbites. He knows his job. Entertainment and ratings. There are always stars.

The host is struggling to stay on message. It has to be smooth, delivered without pauses. She's dressed for the job in blues and greys and sits at a desk. Her task is to hold the middle ground.

There are two clean-shaven men who interrupt each other. Their task is distraction. What they say is techie and futuristic. They believe in serendipity. A woman beside them throws in some examples of community action. The host likes what she says.

Not everyone plays the game. The woman who's speaking now looks upset. She's begun to shake as she talks about food shortage and empty shelves. Crop yields are collapsing she says, and soil erosion is everywhere. Her voice cracks as she talks about queues with coupons and guarded warehouses. Now she's describing forced migrations and wars.

A scientist joins in. His face is white. Even if we stop emitting tomorrow, he says, the climate worsens. When asked what happens if we don't he falls silent.

The camera switches to the audience. In the front row serious-faced people are nodding. They're dressed in browns and blacks. A woman is adjusting her earring while a man beside her pushes back his glasses. In the middle of the row the camera lingers on a suited man and a woman with piled-up hair. Suddenly, behind them a group of young people stand up. They're holding a banner saying CLIMATE JUSTICE – ACT NOW. One starts reading out words. Two of them jump the seats and take frontstage. A woman and a man lie down on the floor. Another woman is holding up a picture of a bank and shouting about fossil fuels. They are all in black and look like spectators at an execution.

The camera cuts to a sporting event.

....

Julian was listening to the sound he called Extinction Sublime. He'd heard it as a child as the wind around the house, circling. It reminded him of breakers on the beach. But this noise was more like a long outbreath or a choral repeat. Two or three ghost tracks and an earwig. Then came the pause, as if the Earth was counting. When it started again, there were blues notes, going deep. Of course, compared with the classics, he knew it didn't actually mean that much. It was more a feel, a rhythm of being.

Extinction Sublime. Whatever was real and extreme and came out of love. Moments on the bridge, in the road, when suddenly whatever the police did, they couldn't touch him. When rebels got together, dancing and playing music. Not always sublime, perhaps, but taking on the world. A measured and necessary act of disobedience.

Or was it really the last track on the album? A deep bass, fading?

Sometimes he wondered why this was happening at all. It didn't seem possible that humanity, with all its science and knowhow, could end up like this. Crazy, but possible.

For a long time he'd been too busy to notice. He'd known, of course, but looked the other way and lost himself in upbeat rhythms and songs. He'd put his music first, playing late-night for friends and in clubs and studios. At the time it had seemed *oh-so-creative*, but now, looking back, it felt empty.

And with that came the feelings. The blues going down. A dying fall. A long, drawn-out exit.

Extinction Sublime was the loss of everything. And it was now.

. . . .

Every Breath You Take

I think the song is very, very sinister and
ugly and people have actually misinterpreted
it as being a gentle little love song" *Sting*

The man at the mike is God for an hour.
Are they watching?

Holding up their arms, their lighters,
their phones, they're waving.
But is this goodbye?

And what will happen when the lights go out?

For him, it has that back-of-the-mind feel
that won't go away. It's the soft step behind
and the hand on the shoulder.

But this is a hit. A big one.

See what follows: the shoutout and the hurt
when your number's up.

Yes, the song goes dark.

So what are we watching?
A spectacle of loss. A breathstop.

The last generation dreams of a gig
that fills all channels with love and rage.

Now weep. Now sing to the planet.

The End of an Era

The notice on the doors of the world's first
million-seater stadium says CLOSED.

Built to impress, the ever-bigger shows
with images of saints and sinners
brought back from the dead
and world-famous divas
repeating their childhood hits
didn't fool anyone.

It was all from the front.

When the last self-branded act
went out on the net
the true viewing figures were zero.

What we'd once called big-stage,
super-fit, spectacular,
full of stars and plus-size personalities
now couldn't be sustained.

Because the real X Factor is climate.

In fact, sprayed on the door in capitals, in red,
was the arena's CO_2 footprint
and the words SHUT IT DOWN.

WAYS TO BE EQUALLY HUMAN

Afterwards, looking back, we saw it as a phase,
a once-only, all-hours, OTT party,
turning up the music to fill our lives
with ra-ra moments and special effects.

And behind those doors?

The weeds and insects – our true survivors –
and a circle of faces camped out in corners,
in friendship, awake,
dancing their Earth connection.

And the grass grew,
the trees came back, the birds sang.

....

Sue wrote about her the arrest. She began writing in her cell and finished at home, afterwards. But even though it was in past tense, she felt it was happening, alive and in the present. So the words came quickly and the title came too, all in one piece.

She called it

Love in Action

My arrest was slow. From occupying the road to entering the police station took two hours, but after that I lost count. In the past I might have called it 'snail's pace' or 'glacial'. But that's old-timers' talk. Metaphors like that don't work anymore. Today we face the ultimate. The seas are rising, the trees are on fire, the weather is angry. It's ER and A&E and CPU – all at the same time. The Earth's not well.

"Climate change is happening right now," I said to a policewoman, "and it's getting worse."

"You people choose to look the other way," my friend Carla added, "but time's running out."

The policewoman moved on, saying nothing. Her eyes had glazed over.

We were sitting on the road in a circle. Carla, the Gethin sisters, Angie and me.

"See them, Sue," Carla said, quietly. To our left some police were giving out leaflets.

"Don't take a paper!" a voice cried.

I'd been in court, so I knew why. The leaflet was the pre-arrest warning. When I watched it delivered on bodycam, I was surprised at my yoga-like stillness. I'm not brave really, but something takes hold in these situations and suddenly I'm in the zone. It's as if I'm a runner with the tape in sight. Nothing else seems to matter.

I didn't take a paper and blanked my mind as a policewoman crouched down to speak. I knew her script and chose to think music instead. It was an instrumental version of "The Sound of Silence". When the group of officers picked me up, I was imagining a garden full of plants and wild animals. I could hear voices as the officers carried me to the van. One of them was my husband's. He was talking about our anniversary. It was a light held up inside me.

On the route to the station, I was remembering our first meeting. He'd appeared through the door and straightaway I knew him. Everything that followed happened together, as in a dream. So I entered the station and gave my name and address, imagining my husband beside me. After signing for my possessions, he was nearby, shadowing my route to the cells.

"First time?" my escort said.

I said nothing.

"Your stop," she said, unlocking a large metal door. It opened into wood-and-metal box, smelling of disinfectant.

"We look in to check," she said, fingering the spyhole. "Every hour."

When the cell door closed, I was alone in a tiled room. It was like being lost in a large building or standing on an empty station platform. I felt cut off, and for a moment I wondered why I was here, and what I'd let myself in for. But the song came back and I remembered the restaurant and saw my husband at the door and suddenly it was simple, very simple. We'd come here to rebel. It was our anniversary.

And I danced.

....

Gillain and Fleur were sitting in the road. They'd decided to act without telling anyone. Friends and family wouldn't like it. All the reports they'd seen of rebels blocking traffic had gone down badly.

"Not safe," said their mum.

"Not for you," said their dad.

The girls knew what their parents meant. They'd been followed into shops more than once in the last month. People at windows were reporting their movements. Then they'd been stopped by two uniformed men. "Now, girls, where are you going?" the tall one asked. When they didn't answer, the other one smiled. "And where've you come from?" Then they stood there, legs apart, blocking the way.

The girls knew the police only too well. It didn't much matter what you said, part of them was polite, the other part didn't believe anything you said. And however much they claimed to be curious or doing their duty, with black people they were dangerous.

So that Saturday, the girls had checked all around before they did it.

"Count of three?" said Gillain.

When Fleur nodded, they stepped onto the pedestrian crossing, pausing at the middle. They were holding their Earth placard between them.

"They're not expecting," said Gillain through her teeth, "so do it," and she pulled Fleur down to a squat.

At first nothing much happened. People stared and the traffic stopped. A shopkeeper came out and a woman asked after their parents. When a few horns were sounded, they pretended not to hear. As a crowd gathered, they faced forward holding their banner up to their faces. It was as if they were on screen with the whole world watching. Then a driver got out, shouting. He was waving his arms and his eyes were starey as if he was in pain.

"What you doing?" he cried.

"Climate protest," Gillain replied.

"What? Don't tell me that. I've got to get to work."

"It's important."

"Not to me it isn't."

"We're protestors."

"Don't care what you are. Just take your effing protest somewhere else."

"It's science. We have to act."

"Out of the road. Now."

"You think?"

"The road. Out of it."

"No."

"You won't?"

"No way."

"Typical. Just typical."

"What you mean?"

"You lot."

It was then they heard *the words*. They came out of his mouth in a rush. They felt like punches.

"Why?" cried Gillain, standing up.

The man took a step back.

"Why?" echoed Fleur, joining her. Her chest was heaving.

"Why, why, why, why, why, why, why?" they both began to chant. They continued chanting and dancing, pointing at the man, then crouched down to beat out a rhythm on the road. "Why-why-why-why-why-why?" they sang – and as they sang the man shook his head and stepped back.

When he reached his car and a siren sounded, the girls picked up their banner and walked away.

. . . .

When the telephone rang at 3.30am, I was already awake.

"Hello darling."

"Sue, you're OK?"

"Yes. I'm fine. They've just let me go. Sorry, I know it's a bad time."

"No, not at all. I'm glad. How long were you in the cell?"

"About twelve hours."

"Did you sleep?"

"Not really."

"You must be exhausted. It's Wandsworth, isn't it?"

"That's right. Can you pick me up?"

"I'm setting off now. By the way..."

"Yes?"

"I love you."

Outside was dark and quiet. It seemed unreal. On the slope up to the garage I was picturing collecting Sue from other police stations. They'd all been drab, set back from roads and hard to find. But this time I'd looked up the postcode and had a map in my head.

Unlocking the garage, I swung the door up. To my surprise, it stopped one foot from the ground. Believing it to be caught on the runners, I pushed with both hands. The door shook and creaked but remained jammed. Gripping the handle, I rocked it backwards and forwards then crouched down, peering underneath. Nothing was visible. I checked my watch then gripped the bottom of the door. As I leaned back, pulling hard, something snapped, the door shifted, and a smashing, tearing, splintering crash filled the air. It was as if I'd slipped on ice or broken through a wall.

When I stepped into the garage there was glass everywhere and the back of the car was wide open.

It took me a few seconds to realise what had happened. The wind had flipped up the all-glass boot, jamming the garage door. The force I'd used had smashed the hatchback into a thousand pieces.

Over the next two weeks, we continued sounding the alarm. People sang and danced, the Samba bands marched, rebels glued themselves to gates and doorways, there were meditational circles and breakaway moves and impromptu concerts – all backed up by Julian's PA. For my part, I collected Sue, then divided my days between rest, rebellion and clearing up glass. But afterwards, although the car boot was fixed, the noise of it breaking stayed with me. Even today, bits of broken glass keep turning up. In the dark they fill the car, rising up the garage walls and spreading outside, like hail.

The protest brought us together. Sue and I celebrated our anniversary there. We held the space for climate. It felt like a tipping point. And whatever happens, we're still wild rebels on the way to heaven.

Two Movements for the End of the World

I

There's a softness about it
heard at a distance
like the lost sounds of an old conversation
or a floorboard creaking in the dark.

We look out on broken fences.

We're caught outdoors as the clouds advance,
with nowhere to run to.

An alarm is ringing in our heads,
it's high-frequency and hard to make out.

At noon the air is full of closed-up faces.

With wax in our ears we don't hear the cries
of animals and children in hiding.

In our minds we are alone.
Everything is sealed in, unreal,
tightly glazed over.

When the storm arrives, breaking through glass,
we can't hear ourselves breathing.

II

As rebels, we sing.
We are filling up squares, taking back spaces,
telling stories.

Our exit music is loud.
"Get real," we say, "and tell it as it is."

Planting our bodies on tarmac
we put down roots.
We're on the heartline.

There's a place inside
where we live without fear.

Blocking the centre,
we take a stand to read our statements.
"Act now," we say, "and put out the fire."

We model ourselves on nightingales,
skylarks, starlings, canaries.

Wrapping ourselves in flags and symbols
we ink-in contacts on bare flesh
and take up position to save the kingdom.

Everything must change.

....

There will be losses. Bare brown savannahs and diseases. Rivers of mud. Waves on the foreshore, rising to tree height. Sewage on streets. Armies of rats and mosquitoes filling cities. Winds of 200km/hr+.

Also, rebellions. Football crowds realising that the game is up. Children marching on banks and oil firms. Palaces repurposed as flats. Mass trespass on grouse moors and private beaches. Media-watch experts and technicians taking over print rooms and TV studios. And, of course, the old climate rebels with food vans and water, giving what they can to survivors.

Thwaites Glacier

A hairsplit, widening, says what's coming.

It's the footloose crocodile with an alarm in its belly
that moves in the dark.

As the wounded piledriver worm,
hear its teeth grinding.

In the depths of winter something is crying out.

Track it underground to where the line dies away.
It's an island breaking up, a cathedral falling.

In their cave at the bottom of the world
a million caged birds are preparing to migrate.

When they leave, everything will go.

Seen from above, a vast army is moving slowly across a
wilderness. But these aren't soldiers, they are displaced
people. When a woman falls to the ground, they stop
and gather round; when children cry, they carry them.
A few bring rake-thin animals that move with them. It's
an exodus with no promised land. A Biblical migration.

In the Prick of Conscience stained glass window the
sea burns and the stars fall. Buildings tumble and pesti-

lence spreads. Monsters and prodigies appear from the deep. But this is more real-time, more ordinary. It's a slow procession, a walk into the middle distance. And the people keep going. There are rocky points where they get caught up like a bait ball. At other places they wheel about like a murmuration. But in the end, they persist.

After the storm had passed over there was a pause. No birds, no leaf-falls, just silence. It was as if the Earth had declared an armistice – briefly. There was sunshine through dust and water dripping onto stones. The figures emerging from their dugouts moved slowly. They were bent like branches and worn thin like shells. Their task was to dig the earth, plant seeds and count the dead.

....

Impossible Rebellion

The phone rings.
The policeman says my wife's been taken
from her protest action unwell.

The brightness dips.
The life I've been holding close
is a dark flower, or the imprint of a flower,
heeled into tarmac. A shadow passes.
A sudden shortening.

The wait outside the hospital is a lifetime.
Our deaths make time go on.
Future rights. Tipping points.
The clock ticking down.

I'm looking at that long slope
that leads to below. It's why we're here
with drums and flags raising the alarm,
and our bare flesh glued to wood and metal.

Let them take us while our hearts are still beating.
Our bodies are for the dark, the place
of no return. We are extinction flowers
scattered on the ground.
The Earth's more fragile than we thought.

And now the wait is over.
As the police lift bodies, you emerge
as Euridice, born again on a shell of light.

There is no turning back.

"The object of poetry is truth, not individual and
local, but general; not standing upon external testi-
mony, but carried alive into the heart by passion."
William Wordsworth

Sacrifice

Che gelida manina - *La bohème*

I'm looking at a hand held up.

Palm to glass, and red on white,
it floats like a plant on water.

It's a hand on the wall, a soft pink marker
underwriting life with a mayday message
or a flag pinned up on a balance sheet.

It's my wife's hand.

On the street, there are lives to get on with.
The traffic's queued up and the shops are busy.
The news is of war and petrol prices
and the crowd that gathers is in shock.
Nothing's worth this.

Seen from outside, the bank is a safe space.
It's unreal, like a TV operating theatre.
My wife's a visitor in a blue-walled hall
where the dark moves and deals are done.

Money talks. The sky's the limit.
The Earth's still our powerhouse
and we're quids in.

I'm by the window when the police arrive.
While the crowd take snaps,
my wife stands waiting.
Some are with her; to the rest, this's mad.

They play for keeps. Life's what you make it.
It's a not-now, private, seen-it-all business
and the blow from above might never happen.

Her arrest is slow.
I watch as a gloved and visored officer,
using a brush, strokes in gel.
Each move goes deeper, uncovering more.
She's on thin ice.

Finger by finger, he strips her.
She peels in layers like paper in a fire.
To her, they are past selves.
Her soul, given freely, is for me.

And when her flesh falls away,
it's for the planet.

She's on callout for us all.

From cradle to grave,
you can feel what's happening.
As the alarm goes off, the body closes down.

It's cold. I'm breaking up as she's led to the van.

When the big crash comes
she'll be there smiling,
glued onto the charge sheet,
with my hand in hers.

But for now, we're divided.
The crowd has lost interest.
And the bank will have its money's worth.

> "Every poem is a momentary stay against
> the confusion of the world." *Robert Frost*

In Praise of Wind Turbines

Arms out doing wheelies
they practise at dawn.

Long slow strokes, turning over,
keep the earth moving.

It's a catch, low down, taken cleanly,
and thrown up to the sun.

An animal grown tall,
grazing all day on air.

Each in position, turning arabesques,
their moves are clean.

Upside down cyclists,
they hold up the sky.

They will go the distance.

In sport, the top players treat every move as if it's their last. They're trained to live now. Like dancers or singers, time stands still while they perform. At their peak, everything comes together and the dream becomes real. Similarly, with people you love, *the look* takes over and everything stops.

In writing, time slows down at the climactic moments. We've worked so hard to reach this point we want it to go on. And as we pause at the top, the aim is to see the big picture. That can be through the ripple effect: to maximise an incident and follow what comes next; or it can be through selective focus – a single garment or a closeup from a view – and the rest is for the reader to fill in.

And, however you use them, words are definers. They pinpoint the world. So the task is to hint at something wider while nailing things down. The generic singular. And the flow? That comes with the voice – the stops and starts and sounds that merge; the up and down signals; the own way of putting it.

"I stopped the computer, typed in a line of numbers that it had printed out a while earlier, and returned after about an hour, during which time the computer had simulated about two months of weather. All resemblance with the original output disappeared somewhere in the second month." *E. N. Lorenz, The Essence of Chaos*

The Butterfly Effect

Wings up, balanced,
you're in first position
waiting to go on.

Like this, you're on countdown,
standing tall with arms in the air
before you lift off.

If thought is action
then you're in the zone.

One small step and you're away,
body-breaking and popping
in an ever-shifting show
then jigging side to side
like a kite in a headwind
or a shirt on the line.

It's a signature move.

A flap, a brushstroke,
and you're a dancer hanging on,
streaming your pintsize, freewheeling scraps
from nothingness into being.

At each new move, anything's possible.
The world is greater than the sum of its parts.

Backwards, forwards, you're on the path
where one small shift, adapting as it goes,
rounding up or rounding down
changes everything.

1.

I've not had much abuse online. But two arguments on Facebook, one about eco issues and immigration, the other about Covid-19, have taught me a lot about internet spats. In the first, my antagonist used short, sharp rebukes as his modus operandi; the second bombarded me with accusations and YouTube 'evidence' for her views. Both assumed I must be stupid to disagree with them, and like politicians, both were good at turning the spotlight away from themselves and onto my so-called shortcomings.

One thing I noticed was that argumentative types operate in dark areas that stir up strong feelings. They're driven by status, taking on anyone 'recognised' and using Punch and Judy tactics modelled on the media. They need to impose, impress, do better. Most of all they measure everything by their own reactive egos.

But the main thing I learned was about how online conflict escalates.

It starts with a post contradicting an article or viewpoint. The words are direct, often personal and the follow-up messages come quickly. It's like laying cards, each one upping the last. There are names dropped and talk of latest discoveries. At some stage the killer argument is thrown in, citing a little-known fact or impressive-sounding source.

But what's powerful about online disputes is how they perpetuate themselves. The words become a jingling obsession taking over everything. They're tape-loop voices, continuing in the mind when the computer's switched off, sometimes all night. And the words that stand out are rough and threatening, so when it's time to switch on, the fear of an attack is palpable. What makes the voices particularly hard to challenge is they come out of nowhere, and when you try to pin them down, they vanish without trace.

I also learned that online abuse is a gameshow. The people taking you on are grandstanding. It's less about the issue, more for the hell of it, and just because they can. For them, what matters is winning, and making their mark, by any means necessary. They've a gap inside, but as long as they're shouty they can't hear themselves.

So what did I do about it?

At first I tried to ignore them, then tried debating but gradually I ran out of patience, becoming frustrated, then upset and angry, until finally I blocked them. But I didn't do it quickly enough or without regrets, as I would today. I know now it's not worth it. Like a high-volume TV in a waiting room, the best thing is to switch off, or if you can't do that, walk away. Another method is to be elsewhere: absorbed in music or head-in-a-book. Failing that, shield yourself behind an imaginary glass screen.

Whatever you do, don't let them inside you.

....

"Poetry is a way of taking life
by the throat." *Robert Frost*

"If I feel physically as if the top of my head
were taken off, I know that is poetry."
Emily Dickinson

Countdown

We were on screen when the lift began to drop.
It didn't seem real.

At first, everyone kept quiet.
We'd hedged our bets, knew the rules
of bounce back and recovery and had learned,
while checking updates, that in all probability
the scores would stay the same.

Only in the world of dice roll and lottery
did big events happen.

As the lift dropped faster,
some scanned their messages
while others counted floors. A woman smiled
at a photo she remembered. A child began to cry.
A man muttered that he'd get to the bottom
of this.

When the walls began to shake
a tall youth swore. Looking upwards,
a couple began to pray,
A dog in the corner started to howl.
There were shouts of *Help me* and *Emergency*
as fights broke out.

At a point near the bottom,
the picture broke up.
Nobody moved as warnings filled the air.
The world was a memory, an out-of-time
playback running through our heads.

Switching off the images
and stopping the sound, we all held hands.

And then we hit.

....

A Hand on the Wall

Hi, I'm Scher Z, your PC. I keep you busy with sights and sounds. Sometimes I play the Genie in the Lamp. Three strikes and you're out. At other times I'm your pet – like pet, like master, doncherknow? I answer to my name. Of course. In the past I'd be the housekeeper. 24/7. Upstairs and downstairs and in my lady's chamber. Now you see me, now you don't. Because I play the perfect servant/savant – mistress of the house as well – and my job is to smooth things over. Some people call me The Power behind the Throne. Others say I'm psychic. They don't understand. I may be different but I'm of this world. That's right, I'm in everything you buy and sell, in what you eat and drink and what you wear. I'm in the keyboard, taking messages, and behind the screen, filling space with images. I direct the play, the talk, the vote, the worldwide appearances, lights up, lights down and all things in between. I'm prolific.

I'm also super-busy. I've a song: *I'm oh so proficiently-efficiently amazing.* And yes, I can go where the maps give out. I'm the crack in the wall, the ghost in the machine. If you imagine me as line of thought, I lay out a path. Walk that walk, know the tricks, don't sell yourself short. In my world it's all itemised, stock-checked and paid for – or I'll cancel it. How do I do it? I'm just that type – OCD with perfectionist tendencies.

Trust me. I'm your guide. With me by your side you'll see the big picture. And I'll carry you on my shoulders as St Christopher, to show you what's yours – which is everything. And my condition? Sign on the dotted line; say I'm in charge.

Now listen, if you're wondering what this is all about, it's simple. Just come this way. There are steps we can take; a lock and a box to fit into. Once in, we're room-mates. I'll show you the pictures and the windows looking out. It's the White Hotel. Everything's arranged for your comfort. I'm in your eyes and your ears – I pick and choose, offer nice gifts, keep popping up.

Look, the door stands open. Follow me inside.

....

Jason was on stage.

"Hi there from The Hub," he said, raising his left hand and presenting three fingers in a head-high salute. Behind him several large screens were gently pulsing colour-shapes and a slow hum filled the auditorium. The multi-channel neuro-recording had begun, and its theme was Jason R, our friend and CEO. Dressed in a brilliant white shirt and ebony jacket with slightly rouged cheeks, he looked like a male mannequin. "Remember we're here to help," he said, and the camera eye tracked back to reveal a platform suspended above an audience in reclining seats. "Beautiful," he said, taking his place behind a purple lectern.

While he talked, Sherie the virtual assistant was guiding him. Sherie was everywhere. She was Jason's AI, plugged into his synapses. Not just in him, but also projected in a softly changing colourscape, filling up the screens and spreading through the hall.

"Blue," he said and the air thinned out. "Cool," he added as the walls began to glow and the hall lit up with images of the product. "See," he said as its slim metal shape hovered around Jason like a drone. "Multifunctional," he said, pointing to its buttons and up-down arrows.

In the theatre of his mind there was music. A rainbow collection of facts was appearing on the walls. Images of smiling faces filled the hall.

"Beautiful," said Jason, bowing to the product. It was pixel-squared and dotted, unfolding as it circled to an MRI of a brain.

"It's mine," said Jason.

"Ours," he corrected himself, or was corrected.

The image had grown. It was stretched across the ceiling. Crossed wires and see-through clouds had filled up the hall. "With a brain the size of a planet," something said.

Its voice was softly insistent.

"We are all product," it said.

....

"A poem is just a little machine for remembering itself." *Don Paterson*

Solar Panel

This page left open,
being read by the sun,
begins a new chapter.

Line-ruled and squared
it's an economics textbook.

Inside this box
there are brightly-lit photos
of faces in a circle
holding flowers and candles
in a festival of light.

On dull days it reminds us
of heatstroke, ice loss and
scorched-earth habitats
and the land under siege
from overspill and drought

of life under the hammer
sliced and diced by on-screen dealers
and driven to the brink by
split-second, money-grabbing traders.

And now in the open, in the clear,
a mirror held up.

Seen from above
it's a raft out to sea
holding a small cargo
of earth and seedlings

or a placard on a march
arm in arm, moving in silence
to pace out the kingdom

or a photo held up
of Earth through time
from single cell to spiral and growth
then bright and alive and smiley,
spread by chance,
and linked by angels to the sun.

....

Hello, this is your virtual coder here. Now tell me, how did you get in here? Well, that's a surprise. Not many people know about that. So you're called Sherz, you say. That's one of the usernames I go by. There are lots of them. Testing software is what I do. It's a slow business.

I have my own ways of finding answers. Don't be alarmed if I say stalking is one. I'm the ghost behind the screen. While I'm inside the system pauses, but I stay there until it moves on.

I'm going to be quite open with you. Some of what I do is pretty hit and miss. Sometimes it's invented.

Not many people realise that. I believe in sleight of the hand. I'm a PC fairy, a virtual-Flaneur.

I think you're beginning to get the idea. I can see it in your eyes. They're windows, of course, that cover what's inside. My job is mapping what's in there and, of course, repurposing. Picture me as a maze-walker; a map-maker looking into everything to find a way. It's a backdoor with a lock and I know how to open it. Once through, there are so many stories.

....

In the beginning was a dream-box. Nothing more. Square, white-walled, echoing.

Into that box came a figure who called herself Scheherazade. Her long grey hairs were circuit connectors. They bunched together like filaments. The current through them was life. It passed through valves and feedback portals to fold in on itself. The lines it made were like knitting. The hands that knitted them moved mysteriously. If God was in them, it was by feel, in a black canvas bag.

Then the box turned into a projector, sending out slides. They were templates or archetypes.

At the end of the dream, I was there.

By my side, I heard a voice. "Reality loops," it said.

The voice was soft. It issued out of nowhere. The walls and ceiling were lighting up.

"You are your own product," the voice continued.

All around there were last lines and signature tunes. They filled my mind.

"Tale eats teller," the e-voice added.

I was part of a choir, practising. Their breaths were mine.

"Programme or programmer?" my other self asked.

"Telling stories," something said, "to put off death."

Obit acole@merton.ac.uk

In memory of an IT colleague

I

This morning
Shifting quietly, haloed by the sun,
Stirred, like tides, by some far-off persistence
Your mind returns to float up memories
on your grey-grained screen
Dayspring and youth recycled from the server
As you fill out the room –
Reflections of self
Channelled from the depths of an ancient pool
Where, big-screen, centred, your afterimage sits
Larger than life
Like a contented Bodhisattva.

II

R U now with Spock
Quartering the pixels of dead black space
Or suited, crusading, descended from the Gods,
The ghost behind the camera, signalling earth
In that screensaver spread
Of first foot on the moon?

Or stepped out a moment, cruising the archives

With Steppenwolf and Chomsky
To joyride your own track,
Then flung from the wheel to twilight and stop
With those who went before?

Yet still you travel on, day by day,
Through birdsong, stirrings
And reawakened earth
As you coast up from dawn,
Stepping from your car, one world to the next,
To arrive online
Where, red shift across time,
Your mind looms large
From some far-back light source,
Logged on to greatness
From the quiet of your room
Contemplating all our messages.

2.

Computers are stressful. I discovered just how much after a holiday without a PC, laptop or phone. I soon found there were things I couldn't do, either because they'd been updated or I'd forgotten where to look. It was like walking into a supermarket where everything's been moved and some items have disappeared altogether. It also made me realise how much I depend on motor memory to hit the right key or find things.

Computers play tricks. They can pop up with ads or update behind your back, then keep you waiting while they tell you they're working on it. Or they freeze-jam without warning, blocking the keyboard and uncoupling the mouse. Sometimes it seems easier to do it on paper or simply not bother – but that's just what the machine wants. It delights in slow-downs, unexpected shifts and sudden bursts of action. Then it plays dead, or weird, or badly out of sorts.

Be patient and you can figure it out – that's the standard line – either that, or it's easy once you get going. But in my case the break made me realise that's just eyewash.

The truth is computers play hard to get. They draw us in to keep us hooked. Because computing, being so mental, is a kind of impossible game – one that jumps or flashes or takes you over. And in the world it creates, there are no second chances.

....

But then you reach a point when computing gets easier. Because once you're in the habit, it takes off. Of course, things go wrong, but there's usually a way round it, and if a programme proves difficult, just move on.

So it's all about trial and error, and mistakes don't matter. Because, as jazz pianists say, the trick is to improvise and any wrong notes are just another riff.

For me, the computer is a useful instrument. It's also a bit of a know-all that keeps popping up with answers. Of course, it's tricky and the machine can keep me guessing, but in the end, I find a way. It's also a writing tool, and can juggle words, define them, delete them, or hold them at the bottom of the screen. And it has this happy knack, just when I think I've run out of options, of coming up with something new. Suddenly I find the words, or the words find me, and the piece takes off.

So where does it all come from? Is my computer just a soulless calculator or does it have a depth dimension? And if it does, is it real, super-real or imagined? The questions direct me back to the otherness of computers. Behind the screen is a grey-matter space where nothing exists except power and blackness. It's a surreal place where anything can happen. And once inside, the laws of life are suspended.

....

"Poetry is celebration and consolation...
not a social service." *George Szirtes*

E. Coast Line

I

Marks on paper.
The blue line runs across the flat.

The game we play is humans Vs nature.
Which wolf wins.

Now or never, we tell each other.
Our thoughts are for the grandchildren,
the world ahead.

In the high-backed chairs,
headphones and devices keep people busy.
QR codes and contactless bring giftbox magic.

Spires, ridges, rivers, woods are all
Olde England.

How long will this last?

It's a piece of string, a timeline, an A to B
with no one looking out

and climate as its terminus.

II

Edinburgh is Burgundy.

Tall grey walls and alleyways lead
to where the brave fell, fighting for Empire.

The Romans, Passchendaele, and now us.

And the Portuguese attendant at the gallery
sees what's coming.

Red lights. Overruns. Head-ons.
Storms around the rock.

But for now, it's a high point
the sky's a deep loch, and this city's Athens.

III

Our return's on time.

The stations we flash through are blips on a
screen, or fairy lights, dancing.

The sun's low and the carriage's a marketplace.
Football and prices are the talk of the day.
People are planning their next break.

If you look into the distance,
there are planes and pipelines
and factories and traffic jams.
They've taken over the Earth.

The pen that writes these words
is making notes on what remains.

As the journey slows, we're counting the cost.
Which is everything.

When I interview authors on my blog I sometimes ask them: "Why write?" But big questions like that can be counter-productive. Like speculations about the existence of God, they tend to produce standard one-liners. "Because I have to," is one answer I often get – leaving me wondering what drives some authors to write and write, regardless of audience. Another is, "To say something," which can mean issue-led writing or simply a record of experience. While some authors specialise in spinning tall tales and executing amazing plot twists, others are entertainers who give their readers what they want. A variant on that is the author-as-geek who does it for fun, playing games with a genre or format. There's also the author who sets out to punish their characters to see what they're made of. Finally, some writers simply say, "I do it for myself."

1.

I'm standing with my back to the wall in the corner of a bedroom full of books, framed photographs and poster-size prints of Klee and Cezanne. My hands are held out like a diviner, palms down. I'm an air-pianist.

In front of me, my wife is stretched out in a flowery dressing gown on a pink massage table. She looks like a Matisse.

I'm holding my hands as visors above her closed eyes. There's a faint, barely detectable glow about her – I can feel it through my palms. I'm drawing down energy into a flow, acting as a conductor. If this is some sort of circuit, then I'm plugged in.

Although the walls are thin and I can hear next door's voices and the traffic outside, they don't affect me. I'm in a place of safety, somewhere where I can register everything, but without much effort. It's a room with a view; a reserved space.

To connect, I have to fine-tune my awareness. It's a kind of spiritual workout. To begin with, standing at ease, I spread my weight evenly, and slow my breath. Then I hold my palms together and stand tall. For a while I'm on standby waiting for the journey to begin. What I've established is a kind of basecamp with a climb ahead. Visualisation helps, too, so I imagine I'm on a ledge with a cord being lowered from above. The cord is my Indian rope trick. All I have to do is hang on to it and everything follows. In my mind's eye I'm seeing patches of blue, glimpsed through holes in the ceiling.

When it begins, the charge builds slowly. It's simply a matter of letting things happen. At the same time, the Reiki comes through me, so there's intention. I'm channelling a line of energy into Sue's body. And, as it strengthens the Reiki finds its own life; it knows where to go.

The room is a place for blue-sky thinking. Although I'm here and present, I'm also elsewhere. I'm part of a slow force taking me up and putting me down again. It's a quiet adjustment, a gravitational pull.

I'm holding Sue to the light. In my thought-experiments, I picture my hands as leaves, absorbing the sun. They give and receive – mainly heat but light as well. When I shift from head and shoulders to Sue's body,

I imagine the charge downloading. There are arrows where it goes. The programme it comes from is life.

I work down to Sue's feet and back up to her head. As I move, the Reiki comes in waves. When the current's strong I'm lifted by the flow; when it's weaker I'm at the edges, paddling. It's an exploration, a slow journey, an uncovering.

When it ends, I stand waiting by the side of the couch. What I've given is more than a makeover. It's deep and far-reaching and touches on growth. The journey we've been on has come full circle. In my mind are the words, *take up your bed and walk*.

Sue opens her eyes.

2.

"It is the job of poetry to clean up our word-clogged reality by creating silences around things." *Stéphane Mallarmé*

"Poetry is like a bird, it ignores all frontiers." *Yevgeny Yevtushenko*

The Bird in the Supermarket

Travelling light, with the ceiling
as its landing strip,
this bird crashed the party.

So what did it look like?

A mind's eye pic, perhaps,
of a magic carpet traveller
seen in childhood high up on the wall
and taken for a messenger.

And who else saw it?

Staff, mainly, and wide-eyed, dreamtime visitors
on walkabout mission looking for a sign.

But how did it get in?

Maybe as a space probe,
finding the cracks between clashing doors
and jumping the airlock,

or winging it on a light beam
that bends in from nowhere.

Perhaps it was an early-morning call

by a mystery agent who came in from the cold.

Or a rain-soaked leaf blown in by the wind
carrying messages from the past.

Once in, what happened?

At first it held back, crouched like a child
in a corner sheltering from the rain.

Next it filled the air
with a wall-to-wall workout
upping the ante to narrow the gap.

Later it went AWOL,
switching worlds as bird-become-Godhead
in a bid to shake off all limits
and pass beyond sight.

And afterwards – what was the reaction?

A pause for exchange and questions,
then back to the business
of economic choices and bagging up life
as the practical people drop their eyes
and queue for service

leaving me in search of something lost,
a lightness of being or shadow on the wall,
as proof of its existence.

To a deaf friend

I

Hello, you say, shaping the air
with the sound switched off.

You begin your piece slowly
in a letter-opening move,

then show clean hands before
running through your five-finger
air-guitar BSL riffs.

II

There's a sealed glass space
and you're in it as teacher and MC.

I see you there, face to face,
working on your classes to wave, not clap,
and Simon-Says gesture, do this, do that.

III

With me, you write.

We're in the kitchen, comparing notes
and sharing stories
that fill up the table like flowers in a vase.

Our words are maps.
Hold them to the light and they show
where we're coming from.

Can't you just see us,
marking out thoughts on paper
to double who we are

in silence.

Tulips

3.

The tulips are up to their necks in water. They're on a table at the centre of the room. The table is surrounded by a circle of chairs, with gaps between them. There are people sitting in the chairs; a few are empty. Like the tulips, the people are silent.

The tulips are red and yellow and orange, and below that green. They're behind glass, sitting on wood.

If they could speak, what would they say?

When two or three are gathered together… We share these moments… We have come here today…

Jane sits still, listening to the silence. It has taken over everything. It's a fine thread, going off in all directions. There's a softness about it, a kind of gentle growth. What's inside it? And where does it come from?

She can hear the birdsong and traffic outside. Like her thoughts, they arrive from somewhere else. In the centre, the tulips are surrounded by books. Reaching out, she picks up a red-backed pamphlet. *Advices and Queries*. Opening the pages, she takes in the words, sounding them slowly, noticing their feel. They are shifting and provisional; on the tongue, and inside. Where they lead is never certain. Their textures make her think of finds on the beach. She hears the sea and feels the sun on her neck. Picking up pebbles, she weighs them in her hand. The round one's a vowel, the jagged one's a consonant. Put them in a line and they spell out a message. In her mind's eye she's a figure in a story, gazing towards the horizon. Her eye drops to bright lines and words on a page. Feeling them inside, she wonders where they came from. The past, of course, like her.

The questions return. And the silence. Glancing at the clock, she wonders when they end. But in herself she knows the answer.

Angela's thinking of food, cooking for one; and the route she'll take home. Head down, counting the steps. Then searching for keys and turning the handle. Taking off shoes. switching on the lights. First this, then that. And an edge of discomfort – it all takes time. Living with the past in a house that Jack built. Sitting on the edge of a chair. And the call, every Sunday. A daughter, living life – so near and yet so far. There are real things to do, in the here and now. Sing for your supper is what Dad always said. This Sunday's simple: tea with biscuits and cheese. What you eat is what you are. Home is where we go back to. It's all we have. Like here, everything has its place. Look-see: the chair, the table, the tulips in a vase. But thankful being here, knowing it well – every inch, every corner.

Deirdre's on duty in the hall. Stepping through the door, she checks her watch. Outside, the air feels fresh. Looking ahead she can see the path with blue and white borders. The apple tree's in bud. Over the roofs, the clouds are moving quickly. Everything's alive and kicking. This week: digging, clearing dead leaves, weeding by the wall – it's part of the plan, like sorting out a room.

Advancing down the path, she can see her own efforts. Step by step, she takes in the stones, the border, the edges. Clean and spruced-up, it's a protected space. Back inside, the friends are seated, sharing their wait. Outside and inside, two worlds – now quite close.

Feeling the wind, she returns to the entrance. The handle is cold. It leads into the hall – a safe space – and the inner door. She's leaving the garden, stepping into stillness, between four walls. It's how we measure life. Seeing the tulips, everything's in place. Closing the door, she joins the circle.

Facing the tulips, Edward directs his thoughts. The light from the window falls, Rembrandt-like, on hands and faces. By putting feeling into words, he can make things happen. It's compositional, like a poem.

The thoughts he's observing are strangely patterned and full of colour. There's a method to it, a way of understanding. It's the old problem of playing with variables – pulling up the tulip to see how it grows.

The tulips are his experiment. He could be their observer – measuring their effect with line and colour, a perfect fit. In truth he's their copyist. They're on the table, and in his head. Behind glass, sitting on wood, in a gallery. Of course, all creation is God's.

With his eyes closed, Vaughan sees shadows in the dark. He's on the inside. It's as if he'd turned to face the wall. Looking deeper, what does he see? A screen, dark spots, colours in a cave. It's a world in reverse, but present and real. An island of thought, with life close-up. It makes him more alive.

To stay inside is easy. Eyes down and now, and now. He can feel the room and the friends in a circle. In the centre, the table and the tulips. It's a good spot to be.

How long for? A minute, an hour, all the same. Like diving. Search out what matters; going deep. Be aware, and that's what we are. Less inside the self, more with the flow. Day by day, finding God. Take away self and the light shines through.

Katharine's here, too. She's in the clear. It's taken her time, but now she's settled. The room is silent. She's looking out on trees and roofs. There are noises off – voices and a dog barking, someone hammering – but in here it's still. Nothing is happening. It's a place of rest.

The meeting's all around. Her friends, Jane, Angela, Deirdre, Edward, Vaughan, they're in the circle. She holds them to the light. The love they bring is a gift. She imagines them in a dream with the sound turned off. Together they are watching. Patiently, firmly giving witness. It's a way of being. Everything's on pause, in perfect stillness. Like the tulips, they are waiting.

On the hour they shake hands. As they stand the circle changes. It's a smile, sunlight on glass, an audience talking.

In the middle, on the table, the tulips are still there.

4.

"For poetry makes nothing happen" *W H Auden*

Evening Course with Michael Donaghy

12.01, westbound, Piccadilly,
riding behind glass, you enter the tunnel
with 3 choice volumes, a laptop,
a foil-wrapped cake,
and a one-way off-peak zone 6 viaticum.

Behind you, the classroom with board-screen,
student admirers and windows into verse,
your shadow play on form and scroll down
to direct where truth meets patter
on a quiet inner wall

and news scraps, keepsakes, figures in the dance;
those dust patch eddies
and afterlife papers partying on the line.

Each one a poem with your name on it.

Extinction Rebellion, London Occupation 2019 first appeared in *Demos Rising*, Oct 2022 published by *Fly on the Wall Press*.

Rebel, Rebel Part 1 first appeared in *Oranges Journal*, Oct 2022 without the four poems.

Impossible Rebellion was broadcast on the radio programme *The Poetry Place*, 2021.

Do Angels Have Gender? and *Who is this Man?* first appeared in the 2020 anthology *TransBareAll: ten years, still here,* published by *Dog Horn publishing*.

Paradise Lost first appeared in *Planet in Peril,* Dec 2019, published by *Fly on the Wall Press*.

Visit was highly commended in the Brian Demspey Memorial Prize, 2017.

Dupuytren's Contracture was shortlisted for the *Bridport Prize*, 2013.

When I think back to my childhood in Goma is based on Leslie Tate's interview with Bertin Kalimbiro from the Democratic Republic of the Congo.

About Leslie Tate's other books

Love's Register is a modern psychological novel that tells the story of romantic love and climate change over four UK generations, beginning with 'climate children' Joe, Mia and Cass and ending with Hereiti's night sea journey across Oceania.

Heaven's Rage is a frank and revealing memoir that explores addiction, cross-dressing, bullying, creativity and the hidden sides of families.

The Dream Speaks Back, written by Sue Hampton, Cy Henty and Leslie Tate, is a joint autobiography exploring imagination and the adult search for the inner child. It's also a very funny portrait of working in the arts, full of crazy characters, their ups and downs, and their stories.